For my husband John. I still have all those letters you wrote me when we were dating.
I treasure them almost as much as I treasure you.

Chapter One

T HE LIGHT BELL sounds coming from Lindsey's cell phone every five minutes were quickly becoming a nuisance. She reached down, scanned the latest text message, and set the tone to silent. Rolling her eyes, she turned back to the chef salad in front of her. Her best friend, Whitney, was picking at her own lunch and eying Lindsey with curiosity.

"Maybe you should just message him back and put him out of his misery." Whitney stabbed a chunk of ham, lettuce, and egg with her fork.

Lindsey shook her head. "Oh, no. He doesn't deserve a reply after last night."

Whitney's eyebrows rose in surprise. "What did I miss? I thought you guys were getting along?"

"I thought we were too. Then I got a text from him at 2 A.M. Nothing like dick pics waking you up in the wee morning hours." She took another bite and pointed her fork at Whitney. "The imbecile then starts demanding I send him nude pictures of myself—as if I asked for this entire exchange in the first place and owe him something."

Whitney wrinkled her face in disgust. "Idiot. I mean, you've only been dating a couple of weeks, right? Why would Shawn think that was appropriate when he hasn't even made it to second base yet?"

"I don't know. Obviously, he wasn't thinking with the correct head or he'd never had done it."

Whitney choked on her iced tea. "So, it's over then?"

"Absolutely. These apology texts are insulting. He claims he was wasted and just wanted to show me off to his drinking buddies. Is that supposed to make it okay? What kind of guy wants other guys to ogle his girlfriend?"

Whitney smirked. "The kind you always seem to attract."

Lindsey's own smile held a hint of sarcasm. "Yeah, I sure know how to pick 'em. Handsome, built, and egos bigger than their brains. If I'm ever gonna find Mr. Right, I need to look for a nice guy—someone not too handsome and maybe not so sure of himself. Maybe it's time I look for boring and normal."

"Uh huh. I'm sure that'd keep you happy for all of five minutes." Whitney remarked as she removed her wallet from her purse.

Lindsey frowned. "Hush, and let me pretend I have it all figured out." She pulled out her own wallet, fished out a twenty-dollar bill, and placed it on the table. Glancing at her watch, she groaned and frantically searched for their waitress. "Great, if I don't hurry, I'll be late getting back to work."

Whitney handed the twenty back to Lindsey and shooed her away. "Go. I've got this one. I'll see you tonight."

"You're the best! See you at seven."

Lindsey stood and gave a quick hug to her childhood friend as she hurried out the door of the little cafe. Her office building was only a couple of blocks away, and if she power-walked, she could get back before her allotted forty-five-minute lunch break was over. But power-walking and high heels didn't seem to mix. "How in the hell do those female cop shows get by with such a blatant misrepresentation?" she muttered to herself as she quickly hobbled down the paved walkway.

The wind picked up just before she entered the lobby of Indiana Comfort Magazine. As she passed though the sliding glass doors, she caught a glimpse of her reflection and sighed. Puffy circles under her eyes indicated her lack of sleep, thanks to Captain Dick Pic, and because of the recent wind gusts, she had a long swath of her black curls blown over her head in wild directions.

She hurried to the elevator as she tried to finger comb

her hair back into place. To her great relief, the elevator doors opened to reveal it was empty. Lindsey stepped inside, and once again, began to adjust her appearance with the help of the freshly-polished metal doors. There was little she could do about tired eyes, but she'd be damned if she'd let the rest of her image go unchecked. Lindsey worked as a columnist for ICM, and she'd quickly learned what a backstabbing, good-ol'-boy kind of company it was. If you didn't know the right people, or possess a penis, you were often overlooked for the good jobs. While her boss, George Clayton, never came out and said it, everyone knew he felt women were inferior in the workplace. He also surrounded himself with employees who felt the same. She refused to give the misogynistic jackasses any reason to look down on her any more than they already did, and an unkempt appearance was certainly cause for comment in Mr. Clayton's mind.

She smoothed her black, knee-length pencil skirt, straightened her white, button-up blouse, and assured herself that not a hair was out of place. When the doors opened to the third floor, she stepped out onto the clean blue carpet bearing the white logo of ICM. Her first step was full of confidence. Her second step, however, wavered as her heel began to give way. Before her third full step was taken, she heard a small crack and her left leg was suddenly shorter than her right. Lindsey stumbled at the change in balance as her shoe came apart. Her co-worker Tom Perkins was close by and rushed in to help, happily keeping her upright while seizing the opportunity to grope any part he could hang on to.

Lindsey quickly recovered and tried to push him away. "I'm fine, Tom. Thanks."

He continued to cling to her hip, his hand slowly making its way to her butt. "Are you sure, darlin'? It'd be a shame for such a pretty thing like you to get hurt."

She narrowed her eyes at Tom's face, taking in his developing wrinkles and graying hair. He was only in his late forties, but his lack of self-care was catching up to him. His beer gut pushed past his shoes, and she was being jabbed by something on his belt. *Dear lord, I hope that is his belt.* An involuntary shiver of disgust ran through her at the thought. She pushed back her revulsion and pointedly looked at his left hand—the one with a gold wedding ring that was inching its way from her waist to her boob—and released a hiss through her teeth.

"If that hand reaches its destination, my injuries will be the last thing you'll need to worry about."

Tom smiled innocently. "I'm just helping out. Nothing inappropriate going on here at all." He gave her butt a light slap with his right hand and walked away, managing to at least graze her ample breast with the top of his other hand before disappearing.

She closed her eyes and counted, working to keep her temper in check. It was a technique she'd used often since coming to work there two years ago. Most of the men in her office were old enough to at least be her father, if not her grandfather, and a majority of them were married. At first, the comments had seemed innocent and complimentary, but the more she tolerated it, the worse it got. She'd recently started sticking up for herself as the comments became increasingly lewd and the touching became astoundingly inappropriate. Oddly enough, that was about the time she started getting the crap assignments that no one else wanted. When Mr. Clayton had essentially demoted her to the society gossip pages, she'd protested that it was not her area of interest, to which he replied, "Of course it is, sweetheart. All women love to gossip." It took all of her strength not to deck him then and there. That was also when she fully realized that she'd never move up in the magazine as long as the sexist dinosaurs still roamed the third floor. If she hadn't needed the job so badly, she'd have quit on the spot.

Temper on a short leash, she limped her way to her desk and took a seat, kicking both of her shoes off beneath her keyboard drawer. After depositing her purse inside the bottom desk drawer, Lindsey logged in to her computer and began checking her email. She was mentally reviewing her list of needed replies when a subject line caught her eye. "For Immediate Release: Indiana Comfort Magazine welcomes Jeff Saltzman as new Features Columnist."

The words swam before her eyes as fury replaced the annoyance she was feeling earlier. She didn't need to read further to know that she'd been bypassed, yet again, for a promotion. But that specific decision wasn't as simple as them picking an equally qualified candidate over her. It was bone-deep betrayal.

Lindsey stood, not even bothering to put on her broken heels, and stomped toward Mr. Clayton's office. His door was closed, and she pointed to it with a shaky finger.

"Is he in there?"

The look on her face must have been telling because his receptionist, Kathryn, began to turn her away, then thought better of it and timidly nodded along with a cautious, "Yes."

Not waiting to be announced, Lindsey pushed open his door and barged in. He was on the phone and looked surprised to see her.

"Ted, let me call you back. Something's just come up." He slowly placed the handset in its cradle and smiled up at her. "Lindsey, how may I help you?"

She took a few steps in his direction, then stopped. "You have no intention of helping me. Ever. Why did you even bother hiring me, Mr. Clayton?"

Her candid approach caught him off-guard, but he quickly recovered. "Now, Lindsey, I don't know what you are talking about. I hired you because I believed you'd be a valuable asset to our team."

She clenched her fists at her side. "So valuable that instead of hiring me for the Features Columnist opening I applied for, you chose Jeff? The mail room guy?"

"Listen, sweetheart, Jeff has experience."

She laughed incredulously. "Experience? Despite what you think, I'm not an idiot. I know all about Jeff's stint with his high school newspaper, which was only last year, by the way. He's not even old enough to drink, for God's sake! How can he possibly have more experience than me?" She shook her head. "I majored in journalism, dammit!"

Mr. Clayton stood and reached a hand toward her.

"Honey, it's nothing personal."

That did it. Something snapped, and her self-control dissipated like the steam from a coffee cup.

"Shut it, you misogynistic old codger! I've spent the last two years fighting off ass pinches, boob gropes, and being pressed against the copier by the pervs in this company that get their rocks off treating women like a piece of meat. I've turned in quality work on every stupid assignment you've ever given me. I've watched all you wrinkly ball-sacks take credit for ideas that were mine, and I've never said a word. I will not be bypassed for this job without a fight!"

Mr. Clayton stood motionless, his mouth open in shock. "You insult me. I've never laid a finger on you, nor have I taken your ideas."

She crossed her arms. "True. *You* haven't touched me. But practically every other man on this floor has attempted it at one time or another. I'm assuming you all get a beer after work and talk about all the women you've assaulted that day. You don't participate, but I bet you laugh right along with the rest of them."

His temporary look of guilt told her she'd nailed him.

"As for my ideas, do you recall the cookbook promo we did at Christmas that grew our subscription base by twenty percent?"

He nodded.

She pointed to herself. "My idea. I told Collins, and he said you'd never go for it. Then he presented the promo as his baby."

Mr. Clayton shrugged his shoulders. "It was for the

good of the company, does it really matter who the idea originated with?"

"Obviously not to you. And if that were the only instance, I might let it slide, but I can give you a list of column ideas and features that were stolen from me as well."

"Hon—"

"Don't you *dare* call me honey again! I'm not your honey or your sweetheart. I am an employee that demands respect, as does every other woman that works on this floor!"

Just outside the door, Kathryn leaned her upper body in the doorway and enthusiastically clapped her approval of Lindsey's speech. Mr. Clayton silenced her applause with a stern look. Kathryn shrunk back out of sight as he turned back to Lindsey.

"I'm sorry that things haven't gone as you hoped, Lindsey, but there is nothing I can do about it now. I've already given Jeff the job, and the press release has been sent out."

Lindsey was done. She was tired of his games and tired of being subjected to the regular physical assaults she endured just to pay rent. *Screw it.* If it came down to it, she'd move back in with her parents. "I hope it's worth it, Mr. Clayton." Her words were calm as she inspected her neatly manicured nails.

He looked at her suspiciously. "Just what do you mean?"

"I hope your good ol' boy system is worth the PR my sexual harassment charges will bring this magazine."

His face paled. "Now wait a moment. This is blackmail ... Or, or *extortion*." His waddle of loose neck skin wobbled as he accused her.

Her smile was sad. "No, it's not. It's simply a former employee of ICM telling the truth."

He swallowed, and she noticed he looked every minute of his sixty-eight years. "Hold up," he said as he ran a hand over what was left of his gray hair. "I can't give you the Features job now that I've awarded it to Jeff, but I might have something else I can offer you."

She scowled. "Trying to shut me up now?"

"No, Lindsey. This is a legit opportunity. All I ask is that you let me deal with the harassment problem."

She studied him for a moment, unsure if she should trust the sudden compromise. "What's the opportunity?"

He shuffled through a stack of papers on his desk, then found the one he sought and handed it to her. "We need an interview with Jackson King. His books have been selling like hotcakes, and since the main part of his latest work takes place in Evansville, the owner of ICM wants us to get the exclusive—the man behind the magic kind of thing."

Lindsey frowned. "Mr. King doesn't grant personal interviews. You know that."

"Normally, no, but I heard his publishers are putting pressure on him to drop the reclusive act and get in some face time with the public. My sources tell me he's currently vacationing somewhere in Santa Rosa Island, Florida."

She was skeptical, but a big part of her wanted to do it and show those jackasses she was better than all of them put together. She needed to accomplish the impossible.

"And if I accept this assignment and succeed? Then what?"

He smiled. "Bring me back an amazing interview, with photographs, and I'll create a new position, just for you. Maybe something that allows you to travel the country a bit."

She knew he was trying to bribe her. Travel on the company's dime? But it was do or die time. She needed to prove to them all that a woman was just as capable, if not more so. Lindsey Sparks was determined to be known as the woman who put the men in their place, for a change, and brought ICM into the current century.

"Fine, Mr. Clayton. You have a deal."

"Great. I'll email you the details." He paused. "For now, I suggest you go home and rest. You look tired, and it's obvious you're upset. Take the next couple of days to plan your interview, research Mr. King, and make travel arrangements. We can compensate you for the trip, up to a certain amount. Nothing frivolous, mind you. Just what you need to get the job done."

She nodded her understanding. "Of course." She refrained from reacting to his condescending remarks about her state of emotions or exhaustion. "And to be clear, you will deal with the harassment? It will stop for good?"

"Yes, ma'am. I'll speak to the staff personally."

"Glad to hear it."

She turned and walked out of the door, feeling better about her prospects than she had in months. Yes, she'd been given a monumental task, but she'd also stood up for herself and all the other women at ICM, refusing to let the possible loss of a job get in the way of what was right. She felt empowered.

As she rounded the corner, she saw Tom and his buddy Allan perched on the edge of her desk. "Great," she muttered. Without thinking, she pushed them both away from her desk and bent down to retrieve her purse, her mind on her upcoming assignment. Then she felt a large hand cup her left butt cheek and she froze. Slowly, she stood, and as she turned, she grabbed her stapler, pushing the button that released the hammer from the base.

"Hello, Tom." She gave him a sweet smile. He replied with a leer and leaned into her.

"That's more like it. It's about time you showed me some appreciation. I'm just being friendly."

"Oh, I appreciate you, all right. Would you like to see how friendly I can be?"

"Oh, baby, would I ever."

Lindsey smiled, then pushed the hammer of the stapler against his crotch, sending the projectile staple directly into his scrotum. His howl of agony echoed throughout the entire floor as he fell to his knees.

"You stupid little bi—"

"Ah! Be careful what you say to me, Tom. I simply defended myself from your unwanted advances."

"I'll press charges for *assault*," he bellowed.

"Do it," she said loudly. "And then explain to your wife why we are in this situation to begin with. Or better yet, maybe I should be proactive and just call her myself."

His tear-filled eyes widened, but all he did was try to

breathe through the pain.

Lindsey looked up to see Mr. Clayton standing several feet away, concern on his face, although she was unsure if it was for her, Tom, or his own hide. She assumed it was the latter.

"Are we all set Mr. Clayton? Am I free to go set things in motion?"

He nodded silently as she picked up her purse, stepped carefully over Tom with her bare feet, and entered the just-opened elevator. She turned, and as she watched the elevator doors close, she noticed a young female intern in the back of the room giving her the thumbs up and a long-distance high five. She smiled to the girl and then to herself as she descended to the lobby. The day hadn't turned out so bad after all.

Chapter Two

"**Y**OU DID WHAT?" Whitney screeched as she sat on Lindsey's sofa, empty wine glass in hand.

Lindsey poured her friend a hearty helping of Merlot and grinned. "I stapled his balls."

"Oh lord." Whitney laughed. "I would have loved to have been a witness to that!"

Lindsey took a sip of her wine. "I know I shouldn't be proud of myself, but I am."

"You absolutely should be. You'd be the town hero if word got around. His youngest son was in my class last year, and I did not look forward to parent/teacher conferences. I spent most of my time dodging his creepy looks and envisioning myself cramming erasers down his throat or shoving chalk up his nose."

"Yeah, but you know it'll all be hush-hush. The office will concoct some story about a workplace accident and brush it under the rug."

Whitney held up her glass as a toast. "But we'll always know the truth."

"To the truth!" Lindsey said and clinked her glass to Whitney's.

As she took a sip, she noticed her best friend had an unusually happy and confident glow about her. Of the pair, Whitney was usually the self-conscious one, although Lindsey had often commented on her jealousy over Whitney's beauty. As is often the case of wanting what we don't have, Lindsey would have loved to have been born with Whitney's auburn hair and naturally thin figure. But Whitney couldn't see all the amazing things about herself, and sadly, it often dimmed that joyous light she had hidden deep inside.

Lindsey was just a little taller, and in many ways, the opposite of her friend. Her high cheekbones and emerald-green eyes were framed by long, black curls that fell all the way down her back. She considered herself full-figured and slightly chubby, although Whitney insisted she was curvaceously perfect. Who was prettier was a friendly argument they had often. But where Whitney lacked confidence, Lindsey excelled. She wasn't full of herself, but she knew she was pretty, and she also knew her worth didn't lie in her looks. She felt she had a lot to offer the world, and someday, the right guy. It was just a matter of timing.

"So, what are you hiding from me?" Lindsey smiled at her friend as she took another sip of wine. "You were insistent we get together tonight, and your aura is as shiny as a new dime."

Whitney flashed a dazzling smile and held out her left hand. Her ring finger was adorned with a gorgeous, new, diamond solitaire.

"Holy crap! Whitney! When did this happen?"

Whitney had had more than her fair share of dating mishaps, and after an interesting one-night stand, had finally found her soul mate. Aidan was gorgeous, athletic, and financially stable. He also worshiped the ground Whitney walked on. They were adorable together. And as a bonus, Aidan had an eight-year-old son named Caleb that was in Whitney's class this year. She loved him as if he were her own.

She continued to smile brightly at Lindsey, tears of happiness glistening in her eyes. "He asked me last night, which is why I wanted to come over tonight. I didn't want to rush through the story at lunch, and I wanted you to know before anyone else, so I didn't wear the ring to the cafe. Since it's spring break, I don't have to worry about my students or my co-workers seeing it until we've told everyone closest to us."

Lindsey pulled Whitney in for a hug. "I'm so damned happy for you!" Tears were forming in her own eyes. It brought her genuine joy to see her friend getting the kind of love and life she deserved. It also worked up a small tinge of regret that she'd wasted so much time with short flings instead of seeking a serious relationship. She always believed she'd have plenty of time for marriage and kids down the road. She wanted to build a career first. Sure, she was only twenty-five, but it seemed like it was only yesterday she was starting college. Time went by so fast. What if she worked away the next ten years before realizing she was ready for more? It was why she'd taken things so slow with Shawn. She thought he'd been different. Then he'd drunk texted her and blew that illusion all to hell.

"So how did Caleb take the news?" Lindsey asked cautiously.

Whitney sighed. "We haven't talked to him yet, but we plan to tomorrow." She shook her head. "He's handled this whole dating thing pretty well, considering I'm his teacher and, well, the mess with Rebecca."

Lindsey made a disgusted face anytime Rebecca's name was brought up. It was an automatic reflex from hating the shallow, jealous woman that tried to destroy Aidan and Whitney's relationship before it could be made official. Unfortunately, she had also been Caleb's live-in nanny for a while, and that complicated things a lot.

"Did that jealous hag ever have her baby?" Lindsey had a hard time feeling sorry for the woman that got knocked up by a married man then tried to convince Whitney it was Aidan's child.

"Yes, I heard she delivered a girl last month." Whitney frowned. "I wish we could have salvaged that relationship somehow. I would have tried to be her friend if she'd have let me."

Lindsey snorted and took another sip of wine. "She wasn't about to stick around after the grief she caused. She's better off in Kansas City anyway."

Whitney nodded and sipped her own wine as she thought about the situation.

They sat in the quiet for a few moments more when Lindsey's cell phone chimed alerting her of a new text message. "Oh, for … He needs to stop texting me." She held up the phone giving Whitney a view of the screen with Shawn's name on it.

Whitney rolled her eyes. "Tell him it's over and to move on," she commanded.

"I did! But he's not taking no for an answer. It's starting to look pathetic now. It's not like we're in love or anything." She pressed the side button, powering off the phone. "If this doesn't stop soon, I'll have to change my number."

With a sly smile, Whitney said, "You could always call Blaine. Have him put the fear of God into Shawn."

Lindsey laughed. "Stop trying to pair us up, Whitney. We aren't suited for each other."

"But you two got along so well last summer!"

"We did, for the four or five hours we hung out while you were out snogging Aidan silly in his hotel room."

Whitney blushed. "Hey, it was your idea that I give in to my inhibitions for a change!"

"It was, and you have me to thank for your now happy engagement, so stop playing matchmaker with Aidan's best friend. There is no real chemistry. Blaine and I are better off as friends."

"If you say so." Whitney sipped the last of her wine and placed her glass on the coffee table. "Now, you've heard my big news, what was yours?"

"Oh, no. I want to hear wedding plans first!"

"Lindsey, we haven't even started on those. Nothing to tell yet. Time for your news. Spill!"

Lindsey brushed her long, black curls away from her face. "Well, before the ball stapling incident, I had it out with Mr. Clayton. I learned they gave the features column to Jeff."

Whitney looked confused. "Mail room Jeff? The one that recently graduated high school?"

"One and the same," said Lindsey. "So I confronted him about the misogyny and sexual harassment in the office."

Whitney's eyes went wide. "Wow. You finally did it!" Then she frowned. "Do you need a new job? Aidan might need some help at the sports complex."

"That's the big news. I laid him out, and instead of firing me, he offered me a big story. An almost impossible story, but a big one nonetheless."

Whitney clapped her hands excitedly. "That's fantastic!"

"Yeah, but there is a catch. I have a limited budget to make this happen, and it turns out my assignment is in Santa Rosa Island, Florida." She paused a minute. "So … I was wondering if I could borrow Aidan's beach house down there. I remember you mentioning one somewhere in the area. That'd save me a ton of money if I didn't have to rent a room."

Whitney nodded thoughtfully. "I'll check with him in the morning. I know that his brother, Jay, stays there sometimes, when he's not meandering all over the country with his sculptures, but as far as I know, the house is vacant right now."

Lindsey pulled her friend in for another hug. "Thank you so much. Even if Aidan says no, I appreciate the effort."

Whitney returned the embrace, then leaned back and smiled. "Things are looking up for us both, I think."

"I believe you're right." She just hoped it wasn't the proverbial calm before the storm.

Lindsey sat at her table with a bagel in one hand while her other hand used the mouse to scroll through flight options. She was working hard not to choke on her breakfast as she took in the current airline fees. The flight was going to cut a huge chunk out of her travel budget. If Aidan couldn't loan her the beach house, she was screwed. A part of her felt sure that the restricted budget was nothing more than an attempt on Mr. Clayton's part to make a difficult job even harder. If she could only afford to stay somewhere for a few days, locating and convincing Mr. King to do an interview could prove a tougher job than she imagined. At that point, all she knew was he was vacationing in the general area. It was up to her to put the rest of the plan in motion. She'd put in a call to his representatives, but as expected, they were very tight-lipped about his exact location. A Mr. Matthis confirmed that King was vacationing in Florida, but said he'd have to get back to her on the interview request.

She'd already researched possible resort areas where high-profile clients were assured privacy from the general public. There were two or three that seemed very much like his sort of place. Not that she knew much about him, thanks to his eccentricities and overall avoidance of the press. What she did know was that he was male, wrote two best sellers in a row, and hated being in the public eye. No one had photos of him and his agent and publishing house had to agree to his odd terms before signing him on as a client. She'd also read part of his first book, and while she was enjoying it so far, she also felt his story arcs were a tad overdone. Or it could have been that spy thrillers and crooked politicians weren't that interesting to her. Either way, she certainly didn't see evidence in his work that suggested he'd earned such an inflated ego.

She reluctantly booked her flight out, leaving her return flight open to adjustment. She left in two days. Two days to get a plan together that would lure Mr. King from his hiding spot and grant her an interview. While she'd always been self-assured and confident, she had to admit the assignment was causing small ripples of anxiety. *What if I fail? No, I won't. That's not an option.*

She was giving herself a pep talk when her doorbell rang. Moving swiftly to the door, she opened it to find Whitney, Caleb, and Aidan on the other side. Caleb ran straight to her and gave her a big hug.

"Aunt Lindsey! Guess what? I have good news!" He jumped up and down excitedly.

"What's up, little man?" She smiled at him as she bent down to meet his eyes.

"My dad is gonna marry Whitney! I'm gonna have a mom again!" His smile was ear to ear, and the joy radiating from his face assured her that he'd have no trouble adjusting to his new home life.

"That's the best news *ever*," Lindsey shouted as she gave him a high five.

He bounced around the room as Whitney and Aidan moved closer to accept congratulatory hugs from her.

"I'm so glad you all came over this morning to share the good news." She smiled at Aidan and he winked at her. In a softer voice, she said, "And I'm very glad Caleb is so happy that Whitney said yes."

Aidan pulled Whitney to his side and kissed her temple. "He's not the only one."

Whitney blushed, then pulled him with her to the sofa. Taking a seat, she smiled at him. "You have something for Lindsey, right?"

Aidan looked confused for a moment and Lindsey laughed. "If it's a ring, I gotta tell ya that I'm not into the polygamy thing."

He laughed as he realized that Whitney had changed subjects on him. "No, not that. But she's right, I do have something for you." He pulled an envelope out of his jacket pocket and handed it to her.

She opened the flap to find a set of keys and directions to his beach house. "Oh, thank you," she squealed as she leaned forward and hugged them both. "I promise to take good care of the place for you and leave it just as I found it."

"I'm glad to help." He made a frustrated face. "Hopefully, Jay left it in good shape when he took off for Chicago last month. You'll probably at least need to make a grocery run for basics. His communication sucks lately, but last time we talked he said his tour schedule has him roaming all over the northern part of the country, so we probably won't hear from him again for a couple of months."

Lindsey frowned. "Do you worry about him with all that traveling?" She motioned for Caleb to come sit next to her, and he settled himself in-between her and Whitney.

Aidan nodded. "I call to check on him now and then, but most of the time I get his voice mail. He's not reliable when it comes to calling people back."

She shook her head. "What is it about creatives and their eccentricities?"

Whitney laughed. "Aren't you a creative, being a writer?"

"It's not quite the same, smart-ass." She cringed when she realized she'd just cursed in front of Caleb. "Sorry Caleb, don't say that, okay?"

He looked confused. "Why, is it bad to be smart?"

"No, not the smart part, the …" It dawned on Lindsey that to explain, she'd have to say "ass" again. She looked at Whitney for help.

Amy Hale

"I'll explain it later, Caleb. Just keep in mind never to repeat things Aunt Lindsey says since she has a potty mouth."

He nodded, and Whitney elbowed Aidan for laughing.

"Anyway," Lindsey began again, "I don't use words to create fictional worlds, mold clay into recognizable items, or turn blank canvas into masterpieces. I just organize facts into understandable sentences."

Aidan grinned at her. "Somehow, I think you do make masterpieces, in your own way."

Lindsey shook her head. "If you weren't already taken …" She winked at Whitney. "Maybe I should rethink that polygamy thing after all?"

"Oh no! One feisty woman is enough for me, thank you."

They all laughed, and Caleb frowned.

"Aunt Lindsey, what is a polygamy?" he asked in complete innocence.

She put her hands in her face.

Whitney sighed. "Maybe we should go before Aunt Lindsey opens her mouth again."

They all stood, and Aidan turned to Lindsey. "Stay at the beach house as long as you need. It'll be a great place to relax, as well as work. I think the time away will be good for you."

She nodded in appreciation. "Thank you. I hope you're right."

Chapter Three

LINDSEY CLOSED THE trunk of her rental and smiled at the mild humidity and sunshine that surrounded her. Sure, it was different than Indiana, but that was why she loved it. March at home meant dealing with ever-changing weather. It wasn't uncommon to need the heater in the morning and then use the air conditioner by midafternoon. She was more than ready for a tropical setting. Even though it wasn't a vacation, she was staying in a house right off of the beach. She felt it'd be a crime not to enjoy the sand and surf a little while she was there.

As Aidan had said, it'd be good to relax.

She adjusted the seat and punched the address into the vehicle's navigation system. Once she was settled, she set out on the highway to enjoy the scenic drive that would ultimately take her to her new home for the next week or so. She smiled as she saw palm trees instead of evergreens, and winter coats were replaced by shorts and t-shirts. "I could certainly get used to this," she said to herself as she passed snack shacks, surf shops, and kiosks advertising island tours. The closer she got to the ocean, the more she felt herself unwind. She realized the little change of scenery was exactly what she needed. The sand and tide were a vast improvement over a desk and the stark grey walls of her office environment.

As she pulled onto the small paved road that belonged exclusively to Aidan's house, she realized just how far off the beaten path she'd come. She could easily see why Aidan loved to visit as often as he could. Palm trees flocked each side of the path leading up to the house. Exotic-looking flowers bloomed everywhere, and when the wind blew just right, their scent was intoxicating. The house itself looked like something out of a magazine. The first thing she noticed was the open porch that wrapped around the house. A variety of seating options were strategically placed for the best view of the area and maximum comfort. The slate-blue siding was in vibrant contrast to the bright white trim, shutters, and picket fencing that framed in the two-story cottage. She couldn't wait to see the side facing the ocean. Lindsey just knew it'd be a great place to write up her interview, once she figured out how to achieve the unachievable. But she was resolved to keep an open and positive mindset. She'd find a way to convince Mr. King to agree to an interview and she couldn't wait to see Mr. Clayton's shocked face when she handed him the story of the year.

She parked her car near the front door, bypassing the detached garage nearby. Once she'd removed her suitcase from the backseat, she strolled up the walkway leading to the front door and inserted her key in the lock. With one turn of the knob, she was inside and already in love with the house. She took a quick turn around the bottom floor to get a feel for the layout. Finding the French double doors that led to the private beach, she decided the upstairs could wait. She'd relax with a serene walk on the beach, clear away the jet-lag as well as her muddled thoughts, and then get to work. She picked a bedroom to her right and changed into her bathing suit, leaving her suitcase and purse near the bed. She put on a white gauzy sarong and picked up a towel she found the immaculate adjoining bathroom, just in case the water was warm enough to take a dip. Then she slowly made her way to the waves that called to her. The warm white sand felt good beneath her bare feet, and she knew the water would be refreshing and invigorating, even if was only lapping at her toes.

An hour later, Lindsey retied her sarong around her waist and slowly made her way back to the house. She smiled as she walked, taking note of every detail she passed. The sand, the rocks, plant life—everything felt perfect. And the solitude was amazing. Not a sound outside of nature could be heard. The waves crashing softly were the perfect background music to start her new adventure. She pulled open the French doors and stepped inside the cottage. Then she froze in place. She heard humming. Masculine humming. It was coming from the vicinity of the kitchen.

At that moment, a man walked through the doorway with a knife in one hand. His piercing blue eyes met hers, and he stopped in his tracks. She let out a scream and grabbed the nearest thing she could find, which turned out to be a small potted plant. Lifting it over her head, she flung it at the intruder. He ducked just as it smashed against the wall next to him.

"*Get out,*" she screamed. "*Get out. Get out. Get out.*"

"*Lady. Hold up a minute,*" the stranger yelled back. He quickly glanced at the remnants of the plant, disapproval on his face.

"I'm going to call the cops. I'll have you put away for *life*. Get out of this house, you *sicko*." She ran for the bedroom that she'd left her bags in, hoping she could shut him out and get to her cell phone.

He got there first and blocked the door. "Calm down."

"*Calm down?*" she screeched as her eyes jumped from his to the knife still in his hand. She backed up as she blindly searched for something else to throw at him, and her hand landed on a small glass paperweight. She lobbed it at him, and his reflexes weren't quite quick enough. It nailed him in the chest.

"Argh … Dammit! Stop *throwing* things at me." He rubbed the spot where she'd hit him.

"If you think you can just waltz in here and … and … assault me, I'll have you know that I will not go down without a fight." Her tone was full of determination, but she was sure he could see the fear in her eyes.

"What are you talking about?" He held up his hands and only then seemed to realize he was holding a large kitchen knife. He looked back at her. "I'm gonna put the knife down and we will talk like rational adults, okay?"

She backed away from him several more steps before swallowing and giving him a reluctant nod.

He placed the knife on the table to his left, keeping his eyes on her the whole time. "Now, why are you yelling at me like a deranged banshee?"

"Why am I …" His description set her teeth on edge and her anger flared. "Listen, Bucko, I'm not an easy target, so don't think you can smooth talk me or trick me into letting my guard down. And insulting me sure as hell won't get you anywhere."

He put his hands on his hips and raised one perfect eyebrow. "You listen, sweet cheeks, your virtue is safe. I don't have to resort to forcing a woman if I'm in need of intimate company." He took a moment to admire her red bikini and see-through sarong. "I mean, you're hot and all, but don't flatter yourself."

She opened her mouth for a witty retort, but all that escaped was air. For a moment, she was actually speechless, and that didn't happen often. That moment quickly passed. "Why did you have a knife?"

He looked at her like she was an idiot. "To cut my sandwich." He pointed to the coffee table in the middle of the room. A blue plate sat on one edge of the table—a large sandwich and a handful of chips covered most of the surface. An open beer bottle was nearby.

"A sandwich?" She was really confused. *Why would a guy break in and make a sandwich?* She looked him over then, really taking notice of him. She amended that thought—*Why would a guy break in and make a sandwich, wearing nothing but lounge pants?* He wasn't just any guy, either, he might have easily been the most attractive man she'd ever set eyes on. He looked to be a few inches taller than her and was muscular everywhere. Not bodybuilder, vein-popping huge, but more like lean cut and definition that spoke of a man who took good care of himself. His face was classically handsome, with an angled jawline and rugged features, yet there was also something about him that made her think of that adorable boy she'd had a crush on in fourth grade. Maybe it was the bright-blue eyes, or the spiky but messy hair. Or it could have been that impish grin that told her he knew just what she was thinking. *Damn, he caught me checking him out.*

She shook off those thoughts and glared at him. *Typical. Handsome and full of himself.* Before she could fire off her next set of questions, he pinned her with a hard look.

"Now that we've established that the only thing I planned to murder is a hoagie, maybe you can explain to me what you are doing?"

She pulled herself to her full height and looked him in the eye. "I don't owe you an explanation for anything."

"Since you are in my house, uninvited, I might add, I'd say you do."

"Your ... Your house?"

He nodded slowly, as if he were dealing with a child.

Lindsey's hand flew to her mouth in horror. "Oh, no." Her muffled voice escaped from behind her fingers. "Are you Jay?"

His eyes narrowed a bit, and he didn't answer right away. Then he shifted his weight to one leg and crossed his arms. "I prefer to be called Jayson. And who are you, since you seem to know me?"

"I'm so sorry. I didn't know ... I mean ... Aidan said the house would be empty. He thought you were still on tour."

Jayson continued to watch her closely. "You're a friend of Aidan Walsh?"

She nodded. "Yes, I'm his fiancée's best friend. My name is Lindsey." She clapped her hand over her mouth once again, realizing she may have just ruined Aidan's announcement about his engagement. "I'm sorry. I probably shouldn't have mentioned the engagement. I'm sure Aidan would want to announce the big news in his own time."

Jayson waved away the apology. "Don't worry about it." He bit his bottom lip and studied her a moment. "So, Aidan didn't know I'd be here, which makes sense because he doesn't know my schedule, and he rented the house to you?"

"In a manner of speaking, yes. I'm working in the area for a short time and needed a place to stay."

"Hmm … this does create a situation. I came here to work as well."

Lindsey remembered the conversation about Jay, or rather Jayson's, odd creative process and realized it made total sense for him to be here. That kind of atmosphere was perfect for finding your inner muse.

"I'm so sorry to intrude on your privacy. I know you have specific requirements while you create. But if you'll allow me a few moments of your time, I'm sure we can come to some kind of arrangement that will work for both of us."

He moved to the sofa, sat down in front of his sandwich, then picked it up. Before taking a bite, he said, "Shouldn't be hard to do. It's as simple as you moving to a hotel."

She frowned at him. As part owner of the house, he had the right, but surely he wouldn't be as callous as to throw her out. "Please hear me out. Aidan knows how important this job is to me and how crucial it is that I stay here. If you want to call him, he'll back up everything I'm saying."

Jayson took a swig of his beer. "I get it, I really do. But I have a deadline to meet, and it's impossible for me to work with other people around. Since I was here first, it's only fair that you find other accommodations."

She narrowed her eyes at him. "Wait. Where were you when I was changing and settling in? You weren't here."

"Ah, I've been upstairs all day. I have the entire upper floor as a bedroom and workspace at the moment. I must have had my ear buds in since I didn't hear you come in or head out to the beach. Music helps me create sometimes, unlike interruptions." He gave her a pointed look.

She was trying to be civil, but he was being stubborn. "Are you always this rude to your guests?"

"You—" he pointed a finger at her "—are not *my* guest. I didn't invite you. What Aidan plans has nothing to do with me and my purpose here."

Lindsey clasped her hands behind her back and pressed her lips together. *Of all the rude, obnoxious, pretentious jackasses she'd ever met, he took the cake.* She could see why he and Aidan weren't terribly close. "I can promise you that you'll never even know I'm here. I'll stay downstairs the entire time and be very quiet. If things go as planned, I won't be here but a few days anyway, and then you can have your precious beach house all to yourself again." She couldn't keep the sarcasm from her voice, no matter how hard she tried. She quickly added, "Honestly, I won't be any trouble at all." She stopped herself there. Lindsey was about to tell him she couldn't afford to go anywhere else anyway, but the emotional exhaustion of the last few days was taking its toll on her, and she couldn't bring herself to admit defeat. Not to mention, she wasn't about to let Jayson win the argument. She slowly sat herself on the sofa opposite his and stared him down. Looking back, she was sure she'd decide it was childish, but at that moment, she was determined to make him break the silence first.

He leaned back and set his jaw. He met her stare with his own.

She gave him a sweet smile that was obviously forced.

He smirked back at her.

She adjusted her position to get more comfortable, crossed her long legs, and mentally dug in her heels.

Jayson took a moment to openly admire the view of her legs, then put his legs up on the table and stretched his arms out behind him. He clasped his fingers together and placed his hands behind his head.

Lindsey instantly noticed the way his pectorals and biceps moved as he reclined in front of her, and she lost her train of thought for a moment. She chided herself. *Damn it, girl! Snap out of it. You've dealt with more than your fair share of handsome jerks before. Pay attention!*

When she met his eyes once more, she could see him working to hold back laughter. *Is he laughing at me?* This thought only raised her ire more. Any trace of congeniality disappeared as she openly glared at him.

His smile widened.

She was sure he felt he was winning their silent game. If he wanted to play dirty, she could do that, too. She stood, then walked to the doors leading to the beach and threw them open. After a couple more steps, she was on the deck. She turned at an angle that gave him the best view of her bottom and hips, then slowly untied the sarong and pretended to shake sand out of it. Then she flipped her head down and shook out her hair, running her fingers through her curls. When she stood up straight, her hair framed her face and shoulders in a way that, if her past boyfriends were telling the truth, made a man think of large beds and satin sheets.

She folded the sarong and walked back inside, closing the doors behind her. When she looked at him again, he was frowning. *"Well,"* she thought *"that's not exactly the expression I expected."*

She cleared her throat as she stood there in nothing but her bikini. "Sand. The stuff gets everywhere." He still didn't reply, and she found she was a bit ashamed of herself. *Why did I resort to trying to persuade him that way? And damn it all to hell, why didn't it work?* She decided she did not like the way her mind flip-flopped in the few minutes she'd known him. It wasn't her normal mode of operation. *It has to be the exhaustion. Yes, that's all it is. I'm tired.*

His voice broke into her thoughts. "Fine. If you swear that you'll stay down here and leave me alone, we can try it." She gave him a genuine smile, and his frown deepened. "You're sure it'll only be a few days?"

Lindsey knew she couldn't promise a time frame, but in reality, she only had a few days' worth of budget to keep her going. If she hadn't nabbed her interview by then, she probably wasn't going to. "Yes, it should go by rather quick."

He watched her a moment longer, then stood. "Want a beer?"

She nodded, unable to push her voice past the sudden lump in her throat. *Is he really letting me stay?* She worked to hide her relief.

He left her standing in the living area for only a moment, carefully stepping over the remains of the plant she'd assaulted him with earlier, before returning with a cold beer in both hands. He passed one to her then sat back down. "I assume you have your own car?"

Again, she nodded and perched herself carefully on the edge of the other sofa.

"Well, for tonight you're welcome to whatever I've stocked in the fridge and pantry, but I recommend you go shopping in the morning. I have minimal tastes, and I'm perfectly content to survive off of sandwiches, cereal, and macaroni and cheese. You might want something more appetizing while you're here."

"Thank you. That's very kind of you."

Jayson took a drink from his newly-opened bottle. "I'm not kind, Lindsey." His tone was matter-of-fact. "I'm just a workaholic doing what I've got to do to get through this disastrous arrangement."

She took a drink from her own bottle. "Well, at least you're being honest."

He grinned slightly. "Always am."

She replied with a somewhat self-satisfied grin of her own. "So, you don't mind if I'm completely candid with you?"

"I'd prefer you were." He lifted the beer to his lips again.

"Great. Because I really think you should know that I think you're an ass."

He coughed, taken by surprise at her admission.

She stood. "I expected you to be an odd one, given what I'd heard about you, but I also expected you to have some of Aidan's more gentlemanly qualities."

He wrinkled his brow. "Why the hell would I be like Aidan?"

"Most siblings are at least something alike. But you two? One of you must be adopted!" She turned on her heel and quickly walked to the bedroom that was hers. He opened his mouth, but she didn't let him get a word out before snapping at him once more. "I think it's time I left you to your solitude, Jayson."

Two more steps and she was inside the bedroom and slamming the door behind her. Just before she did so, she noticed his shocked expression. *Good! He deserved a little set down for being such a cad!* She wasn't sure why, but his expression of kindness over the food had touched her, only to piss her off even more when she realized he wasn't being considerate at all. For whatever reason, his rejection of her attempt at friendliness, however forced and reluctant, hit a nerve. It stung, but she wasn't exactly sure why. She had to assume it was pride rearing its ugly head.

She moved to the bathroom and turned on the shower, letting the warm water flow from the various massage shower heads placed strategically along the ceiling and walls. She quickly removed her beach wear, which still contained traces of sand, and stepped under the soothing water. As it ran down her body and slowly relaxed her tense muscles, she did her best not to think of the odd and uncomfortable predicament she found herself in—or the man that was right in the center of it.

Chapter Four

JAYSON SAT ON the sofa and stared at the closed door of what appeared to be Lindsey's bedroom. *What the hell just happened?* He came there to get away from people and work in solitude. One minute he was happy and humming a tune as he made a sandwich, the next he was being pelted by flying vegetation and learned he had a roommate. A seriously sexy roommate, but that wasn't a good thing. She would be yet another distraction that hindered him from hitting his deadline. Hopefully, Lindsey would actually be gone in a few days like she'd said.

He ran a hand over his face in frustration. He knew he'd been rude, and he hated that, but that was often the cost of his creativity. He had to push people away so he could focus and just feel. It was odd how that worked for him. His inspiration only seemed to manifest when he left everything and everyone behind. And his current deadline was killing him. He'd already had to put in two calls asking for an extension. His creative block needed a hammer taken to it, which was why he came to a remote house in Florida in the first place. He needed a fresh perspective and a change of scenery. He had just started to make progress when Lindsey arrived.

He stood and looked around the room. *At least she didn't destroy anything expensive.* Jayson picked up the remains of the plant and threw it in the trash, then he swept up the rest of the mess and put everything away. Grabbing his plate and beer, he went upstairs to finish his lunch and hopefully regain his concentration.

After finishing his sandwich, he found himself just staring at the floor, lost in thought. When he closed his eyes, all he saw were Lindsey's beautiful green eyes, and then it switched to the enticing vision of her shaking the sand out of her hair and cover up. *Why the hell had that made a difference in my decision for her to stay?*

He grabbed his cell phone and found the name Simon in his contacts, then hit the call button and sat down at the desk.

"What now?" barked a voice on the other end.

"Simon, it's Jayson. We have a problem."

"Oh, hey, Jayson. Sorry, thought you were my agent.

Amy Hale

He's been on my ass this week, and I'm sick of hearing from him." He paused. "You said we have a problem?"

"Yes. One with long legs, dark hair, and green eyes. I don't need this kind of distraction."

"Dude, who you hook up with while you are there has nothing to do with me. Although, I don't mind hearing the stories later."

"I'm not hooking up! You know I came here to be left alone. Seriously, you don't know her? She said her name is Lindsey and that Aidan loaned her use of the house for a few days."

"Oh, hell. Aidan only uses the house in the late summer, and he's never loaned it out before. She must be a very close friend of his if he did that. Can't say that I've had the pleasure of meeting her, although she sounds like someone I might want to get to know." Simon chuckled.

Jayson sighed. "Well, since I rented this house from you believing I'd be left totally alone, this presents a problem."

"Sorry, man. I had no idea. I'd be happy to refund some of your money, if that helps. Or you can kick her out. Explain your situation."

"Or you could call Aidan and have him kick her out. This isn't my mistake and shouldn't be my responsibility to fix."

"When did you become such a wuss?"

"Damn you, Simon! I'm just trying to get some work done here! I don't need this."

"My bad. You're not a wuss, you're a diva."

"So help me, if we hadn't been friends for so long

I'd hunt you down and kick your ass right now. Help me fix this problem! She's insisting on staying, and we've already had one fight. She's confusing …" Jayson stopped mid-sentence, remembering something she'd said. "Wait, she mentioned something about siblings and compared me to Aidan."

"What? Why would she do that?" Simon sounded as confused as Jayson.

"When I first met her, she called me Jay, but I explained to her I preferred Jayson. I hate it when people shorten my name. Anyway, I thought she knew who I was. But now …"

Simon was quiet for just a moment, then burst into laughter.

"Why is this so amusing?"

"Because, she thinks you're me!"

"Why would she think that? Your name is Simon."

"True, but my family calls me by my middle name, which is Jay."

Jayson groaned. "Well, that makes a little more sense."

"So …" Simon let the word drag out a moment. "You said she was hot. How hot?"

"I didn't use the word hot. But yeah, she's hot."

"Like Angelina Jolie hot?"

A chuckle escaped Jayson's lips. "More like a real life Esmeralda from that Disney hunchback movie."

"Damn! Maybe I should take some time off and come visit you myself."

"Oh, lord no. Please. Just stay there. It's bad enough having one person here, two will have me ready to drown myself in the ocean by the end of the week."

"So, are you gonna kick her out?"

Jayson considered it for a moment. While he really wanted her to leave, there was something about her that kept him from pushing it. "Nah, probably not. She thinks it'll only be a few days, so I'm sure I can work around her for that long." He paused a moment. "But you do owe me for the interruption. Your assurances that I'd be left alone were bogus."

"Yeah, yeah," Simon muttered. "I'll make it up to you somehow. Now get back to work so I can." Then he hung up.

Jayson sat the phone on his desk and looked around, as if searching for his inspiration. He needed his muse to come out of hiding, but first, he felt like he needed to apologize to Lindsey. He didn't have time for her distractions, but her anger at him was hanging over him like a cloud, and he needed to clear the air so he could create.

Sitting down at his desk, he started to write.

Lindsey sat at the small desk in her room and stared at her laptop screen. She'd made several calls to resorts in the area, and none of them would admit to housing or even seeing someone that might have been Jackson King. She wasn't exactly sure what she would do once she found him, but she'd cross that bridge when she got there. Maybe a casual accidental meeting? Should she be direct? Maybe she could flirt … No, that wasn't truly her style.

Besides, the little experiment with Jayson proved that tactic was an utter failure. Even her assignment wasn't worth that humiliation again.

She was on hold, yet again, with one of King's representatives when she heard a noise at her door. She turned to see a flat white object slide under the door and into her room. Her brows furrowed as she stared at the envelope with her name scribbled across the front.

"Miss Sparks?" came a voice from her cell phone.

"Yes, I'm here," she said a little too eagerly as she focused her attention back to her call.

"I'm sorry. Mr. King isn't currently taking calls. I can leave him another message, if you'd like."

She sighed loudly. "Please explain to him that I'm only here for a few days and would be most appreciative if we could at least speak on the phone for a few minutes. I promise not to take up too much of his time."

"I can try, ma'am, but he's a busy man, and I can't promise you anything."

"Yes, I know. Thank you."

She hung up the phone and placed it on the bed, then walked to the door to pick up the envelope.

Opening it as she walked, she sat herself in a comfortable chair near the window that faced the ocean. It was a beautiful view, and she found it to be a balm on her frazzled nerves. Pulling out a sheet of paper, she unfolded it.

Lindsey,
*   Please allow me to apologize for my rude*

behavior earlier. I'm under a bit of stress and it sometimes makes me act a little irrational. I hope you'll forgive me. I see no problem with us sharing the house as long as we can agree to some mutually respectful rules. Here are the things I must insist on:

1. Quiet. I work odd hours and sometimes I sleep odd hours too. I have to work when the inspiration strikes me. While I do occasionally use music to set my mood, I usually require silence. Work or sleep, it has to be quiet.

2. Temperature. The house temperature is currently in my comfort zone. I like it a little cooler than most people.

3. Vegetables. I cannot stand the smell of sauerkraut, Brussel sprouts, or asparagus. I'm asking, no - I'm imploring you to refrain from cooking these foods while you stay here. Unless you like dealing with a nauseous male that exhibits signs of PTSD, then by all means go for it. I cannot be held responsible for my actions.

4. Please do not disturb me. When I'm in the middle of my work, distractions can throw my entire process off. Unless the house is on fire, I'd prefer not to be bothered. If you truly need to contact me, please leave a note and I'll look at it once I take a break.

If these rules are acceptable to you, I think all should be fine. Feel free to share your preferences as well, although I can't promise I'll be accommodating all the time. But do keep in mind my culinary skills amount to boiling water and pouring cereal, so I usually dine alone. I also don't do windows and on Thursdays I walk around completely naked.

Jayson

She found herself smiling as she finished reading his letter. While he was still a jackass, he was kind of a *funny* jackass, and he *was* apologizing. She supposed his requests weren't so outrageous that she couldn't live with them. With any luck, she'd soon be interviewing King and doing a write up anyway. She wouldn't have time to care about his presence in the house.

Deciding to agree, but give him a little crap in the process, she sat down on her bed and wrote her own letter.

Jayson,

While I'm not one to hold a grudge, I'm certainly tempted to make an exception for you. But you did apologize and you did explain what you expect, so it only seems fair that I accept said apology and relay my expectations as well.

I have no problem with your demands, although I do think your refusal to be in the presence of certain vegetables smacks of vegetative bigotry. And PTSD? Isn't that a bit of an exaggeration? What have they ever done to you? But I digress. I will delay my love of the listed vegetables to keep the peace. As for the rest of the list, it's remarkably much like a list I would have made myself so I don't think there is any cause to add to it.

I should warn you that I am a somewhat accomplished baker and the aromas from my amazing cooking (listed veggies excluded) may tempt you to wander from your reclusive cave at mealtimes. I also do not do windows, and as luck would have it I only wander in the nude on Wednesdays, so the rest of the week is all yours.

Lindsey

She drew a face with the tongue sticking out, and then carefully folded the letter and slipped it into the envelope his letter had arrived in. After crossing out her name, she wrote his name underneath and tucked the flap inside the back to close it.

Hearing her stomach growl, it reminded her that it was nearing dinner and she'd eaten very little that day. She picked up the letter and left her room. He was nowhere to be seen on the main floor, so she quietly made her way up the stairs and looked around. The upstairs appeared to consist of a spacious landing and what must have been a large master bedroom. The door was closed, so she slipped her letter underneath, just as he had done, then quickly tip-toed back down the stairs.

As she entered the kitchen, she realized that Jayson had cleaned up the mess from her panic earlier. She made a mental note to apologize for attacking him and destroying his plant, then leaving him to clean up the mess. She felt like a horrible house guest already and she'd been there less than twenty-four hours.

She searched the cabinets and eventually settled on a bowl of Raisin Bran for dinner. "*Boy,*" she thought *"he wasn't kidding. He has no real groceries in the house.*" She worked on a grocery list as she ate her cereal and considered her next move to find Jackson King. She supposed she could try finding information for family or close friends. Maybe someone would be willing to pass a little info along. That method screamed out "tabloid paparazzi", though, and she really hoped it wouldn't come down to that. *Why did he have to be so stubborn and secretive?* She also knew that those very traits were the reason this job was so important. Landing the interview for her magazine would be a big deal.

Lindsey washed her bowl and spoon, then went back to her bedroom with the intention of reading a little before calling it a night. She brushed her teeth and changed into an oversized t-shirt before climbing into bed with King's latest novel. She'd finished his first book on her flight, and had to admit that by the end, she was pretty invested in the story. The main character, Eli Mason, was a dashing James Bond kind of guy with lightning fast reflexes and a deadly aim. He'd spent most of book one seeking out the man responsible for the death of his sister. By the end, the bad guy had gotten his just desserts, but it ended with the complication of yet another responsible party getting away. Book two was off to a riveting start, but she found herself wishing Eli was a little more relatable. He was too perfect, and in her experience, perfect was actually a disaster. No one was ever truly perfect, regardless of what appeared on the surface.

After finishing a couple of chapters, Lindsey bookmarked her place and turned off her e-reader. She snuggled down under the soft fluffy blanket adorning her bed. The mattress was unbelievably comfortable, and in no time, she was fast asleep.

The rest of her night involved an odd mash-up of dreams involving a handsome spy that looked remarkably similar to Jayson. His heroics involved saving her from a burning vehicle while making a sandwich, then offering her half if she agreed to do some very naughty things with him once they reached his hotel, which incidentally looked a lot like her current bedroom.

She woke up rested, but annoyed. Fantasies about Jayson were completely off-limits. He wasn't at all her type, or at least the type she wanted moving forward. Her future would be with a nice, predictably decent guy devoid of ego or underwear model looks—basically everything Jayson was not.

Lindsey swung her legs over the bed and stretched, then stood and took a few steps forward to admire the breathtaking scene outside her window. The sun was beginning to shine on the waves as they silently rolled forward and disappeared, only to resurface once more and repeat the motion. The glint of light hit each peak for a brief moment before it fizzled out into the deep rich colors of the water and sand. She opened her window and took a deep breath, letting the salty air and calming rhythm of the ocean wash over her.

She rolled her neck to work out any kinks as she made her way to the bathroom, which was why she didn't see the sheet of paper on the floor. Her foot made contact with the slippery item, and before she could register what was happening, she was flat on her back.

Staying perfectly still, she focused on the exertion it took to breathe. She pushed herself through the pain and temporary winding for another minute before attempting to get up. *What did I slip on?* She maneuvered into a sitting position and looked around her. Next to her leg was a full sheet of white paper with a crumpled foot indention right in the middle.

"What in the hell?" she whispered as she picked up the paper and turned it over, finding another letter from Jayson.

Lindsey,

Thanks for being so accommodating, although my trauma involving vegetables is a purely personal matter and I must ask that you respect my privacy in that regard.

As for your nudist day, I'm intrigued by your confession. I'll admit I'm tempted to venture downstairs on Wednesday just to assure you aren't making that up. I would be crushed to learn you are merely mocking my lifestyle choice of Thursday nudism.

Jayson

Despite her aching backside, she couldn't help but laugh. Jayson was turning out to be an enigma. When he wasn't scowling or giving her that look of superiority, he could actually be kind of charming. At least, it appeared that way through his letters. She felt sure that face to face he was probably still an arrogant disaster—one she needed to clear from her mental space so she could focus on the job ahead of her.

Chapter Five

JAYSON SPENT A good part of the previous evening tossing and turning. When he wasn't thinking about work, he was thinking about her. Lindsey was like a ghost haunting his thoughts. Just when he thought he'd gotten away from her, she'd return with a sultry smile and swing of her hips. Even in his dreams she somehow worked her way in and took over.

Around four AM, he gave up on anything resembling solid sleep and got out of bed. With a quick shower, he was fully awake and ready to start his day. Before he wandered downstairs for his morning bowl of cereal, he settled on penning a quick note to Lindsey. Her reply to his first letter left him smiling and a tad aroused. He had expected her to accuse him of being a pig or ignore his nudism joke completely. He wasn't even sure why he'd included it, except that maybe he was hoping it'd make her determined to avoid him. Instead, she'd surprised him by being a good sport and even throwing in some banter of her own.

His full intention in this letter was to thank her for being so understanding, maybe rib her a little about her nudism, and confess that he was not Simon Jay Walsh, but Jayson Conway—a friend of Simon's who'd rented the house to work.

He didn't know why, but every time he got to the part about his identity, something stopped him. No matter how he tried to word it, it never sounded right. He couldn't find the words to make his confession seem less sinister, which was ridiculous since it was her mistake and not his. Yet he couldn't make himself admit the truth to her unless he knew it would be well received. That baffled him more than anything. They had no connection, outside of accidentally renting the same house through mutual friends. And at that point, he wouldn't say she was a friend of his. She meant nothing to him, just as he meant nothing to her. They were just strangers stuck in an odd situation requiring they share space for a few days.

The sick feeling twisting his gut was a war between being dishonest to keep the peace or being honest and possibly upsetting her. *Would she care that she was living with a complete stranger? At least with him being Simon Jay, she believed she was with the brother of someone she trusted. She doesn't know Jayson from any random guy living under the docks.* In the end, his cowardice won, and he elected not to confess his identity just yet. *What could it hurt? She'd be gone in a few days anyway, right?*

He couldn't find another envelope, so decided to just slide the paper under her door as-is. After stopping at her room to deliver his note, he quietly poured his breakfast in a bowl, grabbed a tall glass of milk, and tiptoed back upstairs.

Making quick work of his breakfast, he settled in for a full day of creativity. He'd been working solid for a good three or four hours before he heard the slightest noise outside his door. He witnessed a folded sheet of yellow legal paper slide under the door and drift to a stop just before hitting the leg of a dresser.

Jayson stood and stretched, deciding then was as good a time for a break as any. He picked up the paper, unfolding it slowly as he sat back down. He discovered there were actually two sheets of paper. The top paper contained a letter to him.

Jayson,

> **I originally thought you were trying to make amends for your previous behavior, but I now see it was all a ploy to get me to drop my guard so you could attempt to assassinate me. Clever how your last letter was placed so**

perfectly that I slipped and almost broke my neck. That would have surely been a believable scenario for the police. (If you heard that loud thud around six a.m., that was indeed me landing on my back thanks to your letter and the wood flooring.) You'll have to try harder if you plan to rub me out. I won't be disposed of so easily.

As for my nudism, I can assure you it's no joke. And since today is in fact Wednesday, you may decide to seek proof. Let me save you the trouble. I've included a photo of myself in my hump day birthday suit. (I realize hump day is a totally suggestive usage in this particular situation, but I don't care. I'm still smarting from my fall and I think I have a huge bruise on my pride. I blame you.)

You could come out of your seclusion long enough to check for yourself, but odds are I've already gone back to my room by the time you read this.

Lindsey

He swallowed. Hard. *Is she flirting?* She certainly had one hell of a sense of humor. He really liked that. And while he knew it was completely absurd, he had to fight the compulsion to race out of the door and down the stairs in an effort to catch her au naturel. He smirked at his train of thought. Of course she wasn't going to actually be down there naked, no more than he'd actually be naked on Thursdays, but it was an idea he'd struggle to clear from his thoughts.

Jayson remembered she'd said she included a photo of herself. He sucked in a deep breath of air and pulled the top sheet away to reveal the paper below it. He threw his head back and laughed. It was a carefree laugh that he later realized he hadn't experienced in a very long time. Lindsey had drawn a stick figure with large breasts and no clothes. Under the drawing she wrote, *"If you really thought I was including a nude selfie, you're a bigger moron than I thought."*

He carefully folded the drawing with the letter and placed them in his nightstand drawer. That was easily the best letter he'd ever gotten, and he wasn't quite ready to throw it out.

Jayson turned his attention back to his work with a smile on his face.

Lindsey sat alone at a table in a small seaside cafe that was popular with vacationers in the area. Rumor had it that many of the rich and famous frequented the restaurant, and the photos and autographs lining the walls confirmed it. She didn't know if it was the kind of place Jackson King might find himself while vacationing, but she did know that a publicist from his publishing company was having lunch there, thanks to a slip from an intern manning phones for the day. Knowing one of Jackson's people was in the area gave her hope she'd find him yet.

According to the company website, Kevin Simpson was a nice-looking guy with dark curly hair, a dimpled smile, and broad shoulders. Since it was only a headshot, she'd have to guess at the rest, but felt sure she'd know him if she saw him.

As if on cue, the man from the website stepped into the cafe and waved at the elderly man behind the counter, then took a seat at a booth near the back of the room. He wasn't tall, but he wasn't short, either. She guessed he was around five foot ten inches. He was a little chubby, but not fat, with a small amount of muscle trying to peek through on his biceps. His blue polo shirt and tan, knee-length shorts certainly made him appear to be a man on vacation.

She took a deep breath, then counted to ten and stood. She took her time approaching his table, afraid that if she rushed herself she'd trip and look like a fool. Passing the counter, she gave herself a quick once-over in the mirror behind it. Her black curls were pulled back on both sides and secured by barrettes. Her makeup was flawless, and her yellow floral sun dress was the perfect choice for blending in and enjoying the Florida weather.

She stopped at his booth and smiled down at him. It only took him a moment to realize she was there. He returned her smile with one of his own and draped an arm across the back of his seat.

"Well, hello, ma'am. Is there something I can help you with?"

"Actually, there is. Are you dining alone?"

He looked around a moment and then gestured for her to take a seat. "Not anymore." His expression indicated that he was genuinely pleased that she was joining him. She took that as a good sign.

"Thank you. You're very kind." She carefully sat across from him in the booth and placed both hands in her lap.

He reached across to shake her hand. "My name is Kevin."

She took his hand in hers. "I'm Lindsey."

He released her hand and waved the waitress over. "So, Lindsey, why has the universe seen fit to send such a lovely woman across my path today."

She cleared her throat, suddenly unsure what to say. Deciding honesty was the best policy, she dove in.

"I'm a columnist for Indiana Comfort Magazine and I was sent to this beautiful area to put together a big story."

"Ah, a writer! Wonderful!" he smirked. "Did you know when you sat down that I'm with a publishing house, or was that just fate intervening?"

"Do you really believe in fate?" she asked with a hint of disbelief in her voice.

He shrugged his shoulders. "Sometimes. Not everything is coincidental. Not everything is planned by us. I think fate falls somewhere in-between."

"Huh. I've never looked at it that way, but I guess that makes sense."

The waitress placed two large glasses of iced tea in front of them and smiled. "Will that be all, Mr. Simpson?"

He nodded. "Yes, thank you, Marcy."

She walked away, and he gestured to the tea before Lindsey. "I hope tea is okay. It's my usual when I'm here."

Lindsey nodded. "It is. Thank you." She took a sip of her drink and then decided it was time to get to the point. "I did know who you are when I decided to come over here. I was hoping we could talk about my current assignment."

His smile seemed genuine, but she wondered how often he'd practiced that look on the many hopefuls that approached him on a regular basis.

"Tell me about this assignment of yours. It must be pretty important to motivate you to approach a complete stranger, so I'm all ears."

Lindsey willed her nerves to calm, and she chose her next words carefully. "It's very important to my future with the company that I see this project through. I've been tasked with getting a personal interview with Jackson King."

Kevin choked on the tea he was just about to swallow. Lindsey searched for a way to help, but he held up a hand to keep her back. After a moment, he took a deep breath.

"Listen, you look like a capable reporter. I'm sure if anyone could get Jackson to share his story, it'd be you, but he doesn't grant one-on-one interviews."

"I'm aware, Mr. Simpson, but you know him, correct?"

"Please, call me Kevin. And yes, I know him."

"Then please, Kevin, tell me what it will take to get

even five minutes of Mr. King's time."

He shook his head.

She fought back her frustration. "Please. I promise to be completely respectful of Mr. King and his privacy concerns. I'll even let him read the article first and approve it before it goes to my boss."

Kevin raised one eyebrow, and his mouth formed a tight disapproving line. "I don't know. I don't think he'll agree to it, no matter what you promise him."

"But it never hurts to try, right?"

Kevin shook his head. "Normally, I'd agree, but you don't know how cranky Jackson King can be." He looked at her for a moment more. "Ah, what the hell. Why not. We've been trying to get him out of hiding since we signed him on. Maybe you'll be the one to coax him out."

"Really?"

"Sure. I'll run it by him. Do you have a card or something? I'll call you after I've talked to him."

She quickly pulled her business card from her purse and passed it across the table. "Thank you so much, Kevin. This means the world to me."

"You're welcome. I might regret it later, but I never have been able to tell a beautiful woman no."

She blushed slightly at his compliment, then started to rise.

"Whoa, where are you going? You're not gonna ask for a favor, then leave a man to eat alone, are you?"

She was unsure how to answer that.

"I mean, if you're hungry, I'd be glad for the company, Lindsey. My treat."

She grinned and sat back down. "That'd be quite lovely, Kevin. Thank you."

Jayson was restless. He'd been working all day, and overall he was pretty happy with the progress he'd made. His muse was singing like a bird, and he was thrilled to let her belt out every note. Normally, that was where he'd stop and take a walk on the beach or read out on the deck for a short time to refuel his creativity before getting back to work, but those pursuits weren't as interesting as they had been in the past. He found his thoughts kept wandering to Lindsey. She'd been gone most of the day. He'd watched her drive away sometime around lunch, and she had yet to return. It was almost seven in the evening, and he was frustrated to discover that he was worried about her. Santa Rosa Island was a relatively safe place, but there was always the chance that she could have happened upon some unscrupulous miscreant.

The sun would be setting soon, and he wasn't thrilled at the idea of driving all over the area to search for her. *And what if I do find her and she's fine? What will I say? "Oh good, you're not lying dead in an alley somewhere. I'm relieved even though I've no place to care either way."*

It made him angry that she even occupied his thoughts enough to be of concern. Sure, his muse was working at the moment, but he worried that Lindsey would eventually take over and be the cause of another block. "Dammit, Jayson!" he growled out into his empty bedroom. "This is exactly why you don't associate with people while you work. It screws up your concentration."

He spent the next few minutes mentally arguing with himself over attempting to work a while longer, or jumping in his car and assuring himself she was okay. He'd almost talked himself into looking for her when headlights flashed across the driveway and caught his attention. He peered out the window to see Lindsey's rental pulling up out front.

He walked down the stairs and stopped short of being seen. He wasn't sure why he was hiding from her, but he felt it necessary to assure himself she was okay since she was back.

She pushed open the door while toting a couple of large plastic bags on one arm. She sat them on the counter and began to put groceries away while she hummed a tune. Jayson cringed. She was a vision in her lovely yellow sun dress and swept back hair, but she couldn't carry a tune in a bucket. After just a few minutes more, he was convinced she was completely tone deaf. If she kept it up, he fully expected to later find the rest of the plants downstairs had withered and died of torture.

She walked into the living area, and he took one more quiet step back to assure he wouldn't be seen. He knew he should make himself known, but after her singing performance, she might not appreciate knowing she had had an audience. The kind thing to do would be to quietly go back upstairs. He'd turned to do just that when he heard her giggle. He spun back around and watched her a few moments more.

Lindsey opened a bottle of pinot grigio and poured a large glass. She smiled and let out a small, breathy laugh as she took her first sip. "Mmm," she said as she licked the excess off of her lips.

Jayson closed his eyes. *I did not need to see that. Images like that are not helping me focus.*

Lindsey picked up the bottle and took it to her room, softly closing the door behind her. He cautiously made his way back up the stairs and into his room. *She's safe and she's drinking. Why is she smiling so much? Is she celebrating? Where has she been all day?* They were questions he felt sure he didn't deserve the answers to. She didn't report to him, and he sure as hell didn't need to be keeping tabs on her. His time was better spent working, he told himself.

Working was exactly what he'd do, right after he wrote her another letter.

Chapter Six

LINDSEY SLEPT LIKE a rock. She knew the bottle of wine she'd consumed was partly to blame, but she didn't care. She'd enjoyed every drop. Her celebration was a bit premature, as she hadn't secured an interview yet, but she felt she deserved a little something after the week she'd had. Her hopes were high.

She had just pulled a small batch of cinnamon rolls out of the oven when Jayson appeared at the bottom of the stairs in a pair of baggy gray sweatpants and a black t-shirt. His sandy blond hair was mussed and his eyes were half open. While Lindsey didn't know enough about him to really be a judge, she'd wager he hadn't slept well the night before.

He rubbed his eyes and yawned as he padded into the kitchen. "Do I smell cinnamon rolls?" he asked with a husky rasp that confirmed he'd not been awake long.

"Yes you do. And because I'm in such a generous mood, I'm more than happy to share with you."

"How kind," he muttered as he reached into the cabinet and pulled out a mug, then filled his cup with the freshly-brewed coffee Lindsey had made just minutes earlier.

"Great, he's a churlish morning hater. Why am I not surprised?" Lindsey thought. She was determined to keep her good mood intact, despite his sarcasm. "Well, they'll be on the counter if you change your mind."

"Did I say I didn't want any?" he bit out.

She frowned. "No, but your snide comment wasn't lost on me. I just assumed you weren't interested at the moment."

He just looked at her from under hooded eyelids as he sipped his coffee.

"I take it you're not a morning person."

"You are incorrect. I happen to enjoy mornings. But it's difficult to enjoy anything when I haven't had adequate sleep."

"Sorry to hear you aren't sleeping. I've made sure to be very quiet so I don't disturb you."

"Uh huh." He seemed unimpressed by her admission.

His attitude was starting to rankle her a bit. She had

to fight back her own attitude and focus on being cooperative. "You probably didn't notice, but I was gone most of yesterday. I'll be gone most of today as well, so you have the house totally to yourself."

He peered at her over the rim of his cup, taking in her tan shorts and white halter top. "Is that your usual work attire?"

She glanced down at herself. "No, but today is work and play, so I decided to go for comfort over fashion. I'm getting a private tour of the island while some work details are being ironed out." She wasn't sure why she was telling him since it was absolutely none of his business.

"Private tour?" He waited on her to elaborate.

"Yes, a new friend is picking me up this morning and showing me around. He vacations here often and knows the area well."

"You're taking off with some strange man you just met? Is that where you were yesterday? With him?"

His sharp tone took her by surprise. He almost sounded angry, but that was completely ludicrous. There was no reason for him to get upset at her activities or choice of company. She expected him to be thrilled that she wasn't underfoot.

"He's an industry professional I ran into yesterday. He's a nice guy, and he's offered to help me with the assignment I have to finish while I'm here."

Jayson snorted in disgust. "I'm sure people thought Charles Manson was a nice guy once too. It's not like psychos wear sandwich boards advertising their true intentions."

She was puzzled. He appeared to be concerned for her safety, which was thoughtful of him, but it wasn't his concern. And there was still that odd underlying anger as well. Lindsey decided she liked him better when he was communicating through letters.

"Well, I have some things to finish up before I go, so I'll leave you to your coffee." She grabbed her breakfast and left the kitchen.

Once in her own room, she set up her laptop and typed out some notes and questions she needed to address once she was granted her interview. Lindsey had been seated at her desk a few minutes when she heard cabinet doors being slammed from the vicinity of the kitchen. She rolled her eyes and quietly muttered, "Good lord, he's such a grouch."

Finishing up her breakfast and her notes, she saved the document and shut down her computer. She brushed her teeth and gave her appearance one last glance before picking up her purse and going back into the living area. To her relief, Jayson appeared to have gone back upstairs, so she made herself comfortable on the sofa.

Lindsey checked her watch just as the doorbell rang. She sprang to her feet in excitement. She knew Kevin was a huge asset to have on her side, and they seemed to get along very well. She'd go as far as to say they were well on their way to becoming good friends. He was easy to talk to and she felt comfortable in his presence. It had even occurred to her that, since he was single, he might just be the kind of guy she's looking for—safe, predictable, and confident but not arrogant. Her mind had then flashed to

Jayson, the exact opposite of all those traits. It disturbed her how often he barged into her thoughts uninvited.

Lindsey opened the door, and the first thing in her line of sight was a large bouquet of flowers. They slowly lowered to reveal Kevin's smiling face.

"Good morning, lovely lady. I happened to pass by a florist on the way here, and these flowers were just begging to come with me. I told them they could join me if they promised to bring a smile to your face every time you saw them. Are they upholding their part of the bargain so far?"

She couldn't help but give him her brightest smile. "I do believe they are."

"Good. Should they ever fail to preform, give them the boot post haste."

A small laugh slipped through her ruby-red lips. "Are you sure you aren't a writer? You have quite the imagination and knack for words." She motioned for him to follow her as she entered the kitchen and searched for a vase.

"I'm sure. I prefer my current role in publishing anyway."

She pulled a large crystal vase out of an upper cabinet and filled it with water. "Well, I find your stories completely entertaining. You should reconsider."

Kevin watched her carefully arrange the flowers in the vase. "No. I can tell a few stories here and there, as you witnessed yesterday, but nothing so elaborate as to fill a book."

Drying her hands, she turned to face him. "I think

you underestimate yourself."

He offered her his arm. "Maybe, but I certainly don't underestimate you, Lindsey. You're a breath of fresh air, and I have no doubt you'll be successful in your every endeavor."

She looped her arm through his and hung her purse off of her shoulder. "Why, dear man, you flatter me!"

He led her to the door and opened it. "I do, but that doesn't mean it's insincere."

They shut the door behind them and continued out to his car, chatting about the day ahead. Inside, at the top of the stairs, sat Jayson. He'd eavesdropped on the last bit of their conversation and had become more frustrated with every word they'd uttered.

He frowned and grumbled to himself. "Psh … If he's not trying to get into her pants, I'll eat my shorts."

Lindsey returned to the house around 5:30 that evening. She invited Kevin to stay for dinner, and he gladly accepted. Once inside the house, she quietly started pulling out the ingredients for Chicken Florentine. Kevin busied himself with opening a bottle of wine he'd purchased on their way back.

As she placed the chicken in a large skillet, she decided it would be prudent to warn Kevin about Jayson. She didn't expect to see him, but she also knew that in order to keep the peace, they would need to keep the noise level down.

"Kevin, did I tell you I have a house-mate?"

"No, I don't recall you mentioning it."

"Well, just so you are aware, we have an agreement not to disturb each other. You probably won't see him since he rarely ventures down stairs, but we need to be sure we don't wake him or intrude on his work."

Kevin smiled. "I see. So no yelling, clog dancing, or shooting firearms in the house. Got it."

Lindsey chuckled as she turned the chicken over in the skillet. "Exactly."

"So a guy, huh? Is he an old friend?"

"No, actually. He's the brother of the man that owns this place. Turns out we got some scheduling crossed and ended up here at the same time. It's not ideal, but we are making it work."

Kevin raised an eyebrow. "By avoiding each other?"

She shrugged. "Why not? We don't really know each other, so it's not like we're friends interested in catching up on old times."

"Makes sense."

Lindsey noticed his pleased expression. She pointed a wooden spoon at his face. "What is that look all about?"

"Nothing really, I'm just happy he's not your boy-friend."

"I do believe you are flirting with me again, Mr. Simpson."

"Hey, can't blame a guy for trying."

She grabbed several items from the counter and handed them to Kevin. "Here, make the salad and be-have yourself."

He let out a dramatic sigh. "You do know how to hurt a fella."

"Somehow, I think you'll survive."

He laughed. "I always do."

Jayson glanced at the wastebasket half full of crumpled paper, a representation of the many responses he'd attempted to write to Lindsey since the previous night. Each one started off well enough, but ended up sounding petty and pathetic. It seemed that no matter what he did, he couldn't come up with something that didn't end up scolding her for being silly and making him sound like a jerk. To make matters worse, he still hadn't admitted that he wasn't Aidan's brother. It felt like the timing was wrong, although he had no idea why that mattered. So with each attempt at a confession, his letters were getting more and more contentious.

He took out his ear buds and stretched, deciding it was time to stop work for a bit and get some dinner. He opened his door and smelled the enticing aroma of what he thought was chicken. *She's cooking dinner.* He smiled at the thought. Then he heard a male voice. The same voice he'd heard that morning. *She invited him over?* His imagination took a frantic jog around his head, tossing out all the possible ways the evening could end for her.

His anger flared back to life. Entertaining male friends was not part of their agreement. And he had no idea how spending time with the man was helping her career. Unless she was sleeping her way up some corporate ladder, but he had a hard time believing she was that kind of woman.

He went back to his room and sat at his computer. Jayson had no idea why her newest friend aggravated him so much. He decided he needed a distraction, so he checked his email, which had been backing up for a couple of days. He took care of a couple of business matters, then closed out his email and looked around the room. He felt restless, and he knew his inspiration for work was shot for a while. Not to mention he was still hungry.

Making up his mind on a course of action, he quickly changed into a pair of jeans and a white button-up shirt, leaving the neck open and the sleeves rolled up. He slipped on his shoes and casually made his way down the stairs, whistling as he walked.

Lindsey was setting plates out on the dining room table when she noticed him. She froze, her eyes wide in surprise. He gave her a lazy smile and leaned against the wall as his gaze met hers. Something flickered in her eyes, and he wondered if, for just a moment, she was as attracted to him as he was to her. Then Kevin entered the room with a bowl of salad in his hands and spoiled the moment.

"Lindsey, did you want me to bring the chicken in here too? I …" He paused when he noticed she was distracted, so he followed her eyes to where Jayson was standing.

"Well, I didn't expect to see you tonight." She turned to Kevin. "Kevin, I'd like you to meet Jayson Walsh, the other tenant. Jayson, this is Kevin Simpson, the friend I'd told you about."

Both men stared at each other with odd expressions on their faces. Jayson broke the silence first.

He pushed his hand out. "Hi, Kevin. It's nice to meet you."

Kevin took his hand in a firm grim and shook. "Nice to meet you as well, Jayson."

Lindsey cleared her throat, in what Jayson expected was her attempt at easing the strange tension that swiftly filled the room. Her words came out in a rushed, run-on sentence. "Uh … Jayson. Would you care to join us for dinner? I'm sure I made more than enough, and I didn't make any of the veggies on your 'no fly' list so you might actually enjoy it and I—" She stopped abruptly and bit her lower lip.

Jayson felt bad for her. She actually seemed a little nervous. Did she like Kevin that much? "Sure, I'd be honored, as long as your guest is agreeable to that as well."

Kevin nodded but said nothing.

Lindsey smiled and left the room for an extra place setting. Kevin gave Jayson a dirty look, then followed her to bring back the chicken.

Jayson sat to the left of Lindsey while Kevin sat at her right. Everyone was pleasant enough during dinner, but Jayson knew that the moment Kevin could get him alone, the mood would be very different.

Lindsey poured them all some wine and invited both of them to join her on the deck to enjoy the sea air and beautiful view of the stars that were slowing appearing in the night sky. They sat in the dim light and discussed a variety of topics. Jayson found himself enjoying the conversation, despite being the third wheel.

Kevin gave a sidelong glance at Lindsey. "I'm still waiting on that reply, but I'm sure I'll have it for you tomorrow."

"That'd be great, thank you, Kevin."

"Reply?" Jayson asked, since it seemed the polite thing to do.

Kevin grinned. "Yes. Did you know Lindsey here is a writer? I'm sure you must have, living in the same house with her."

Jayson shot Kevin a suspicious look. "No, I was not aware of her profession. But it's hardly my business, so I didn't ask."

"Yes, she's very talented too. Her assignment here is a tough one, but I have no doubt she'll acquire what she came for."

"I'm sure she will." Jayson tried to act mildly disinterested, although inside he was wildly curious to learn anything about her.

Lindsey smiled widely. "I guess I don't need to keep it from Jayson. I'm sure he can keep a secret."

"I'd wager he can," replied Kevin.

Lindsey adjusted in her seat so she was facing Jayson. "I'm sure you've heard of Jackson King. Have you read any of his books?"

Jayson took a moment to reply. "Yes, I've read his work."

"I've been sent here by my magazine to get a personal

interview with him. My boss called it a 'man behind the magic' piece."

"Is that so?" Jayson said as he took another sip of wine. "Didn't I hear somewhere that he doesn't do interviews that delve into his personal life?"

Kevin smiled. "That's where I come in. I work with Mr. King, and I'm going to get her an exclusive."

Jayson pasted on a fake smile. "How very generous of you."

"Isn't it, though?" Kevin replied, not bothering to look at Jayson.

Lindsey sat her empty glass on a nearby table. "I do have to say, though, I'm a little unsure how to approach it. I'm sure he's a nice guy, and his books are enjoyable although a little cliché. I'm just unsure what it is about him that warrants such a diva mentality. It can't be solely based on his talent. There are far better authors out there that are more than happy to smile for the public and share about themselves. Is he as arrogant as he sounds, Kevin?"

Kevin laughed, oblivious to the hole being visually bored into the back of his head by Jayson. "He's not a horrible tyrant, although he can be a bit full of himself."

"Oh, dear," she murmured. A sad note filled her voice. "Is he disfigured or disabled?"

"No, he's normal looking. Just an average guy like any man off the street. Nothing special at all." Kevin emphasized the last sentence.

Jayson decided it was time for a change of topic. "Dinner was wonderful, Lindsey. Thank you for inviting me to join you."

"Glad to. I hope we didn't interrupt other plans. You did look ready for a night out." She smiled at him sweetly.

"No, not at all. I'm actually very overdressed … for a Thursday."

It was Lindsey's turn to look uncomfortable. "Ah, well … yes." She stood up quickly. "I think I'll get another bottle." She hurried off into the kitchen.

Kevin turned on Jayson once she was out of earshot. "What. The. Hell."

Jayson shook his head. "Don't you take that tone with me."

"How can I not? How does she not know?"

"She's not nosy. And just how did you end up here?"

"It's a long story. Never mind that right now. Why did she call you Jayson Walsh?"

Jayson sighed. "Another long story."

"Well, you'd better fill me in and explain this entire situation … quickly. Or I'll be telling her who you really are."

Jayson glared at him. Through clenched teeth he growled out, "Fine, but not now. Not here. We can talk once Lindsey has gone to bed." He gave Kevin a pointed look. "Alone."

Chapter Seven

L INDSEY STOOD IN the kitchen and tried to gath-er her thoughts. Jayson's arrival downstairs was to-tally unexpected. She wasn't sure why she'd invited him to join them. The moment he appeared at the bottom of the stairs, her emotions became a tumultuous jumble of contradictions. One moment she was happy to see him, the next she was frustrated that he'd intruded on her time and space, especially since he was so guarded with his own. He looked amazing, and she hated him for it. He was handsome with scraggly hair and frumpy sweat pants, but he was absolutely devastating to the female species when he put some effort into his appearance.

Her mind wandered repeatedly throughout the meal. She tried to focus on Kevin's conversation, but she'd dare to glance at Jayson and her concentration flew out the window. What made it worse was that she really liked Kevin and wondered if something more might develop between them in time. Jayson's very existence seemed to douse that flame to nothing but soggy ashes. Kevin was attractive enough, and he wasn't full of himself which earned him bonus points. She wondered if she just need-ed to try harder. Love is something you cultivate over time, so she refused to give up hope that she could find the right guy with the qualities she was looking for. It re-ally wasn't fair to compare Kevin to Jayson. They were very different men.

She opened a new bottle of Merlot and slowly am-bled back to the two men on the deck. As she approached the open door, she heard what sounded like heated whis-pering. *Were they arguing? What would they possibly have to fight about?* When she stepped across the threshold, Kevin and Jayson quickly ended their animated conver-sation and attempted to look as if they were having a ca-sual chat. She'd have to quiz them each later and find out what they were up to. Something was most certainly off there.

"Here we go." She poured herself a small amount of wine then passed the bottle to Kevin.

He gave her a smile and passed it Jayson. "The meal was fabulous, Lindsey. If you ever need a dining partner, please keep me in mind. I haven't eaten a home cooked meal that tasty since I visited my parents over the holidays."

His compliment caused a small blush to rise to her cheeks. "Thank you. I'm glad you enjoyed it."

Lindsey caught Jayson rolling his eyes at them and she sent him a "cut it out" look. He shrugged as if he had no clue what she was talking about.

Kevin drank the small amount of wine left in his glass and stood, turning to her. "Well, I really should be going. I've a few things to take care of early in the morning, but I'll call you as soon as I have some news."

She rose from her chair and placed a hand on his arm. "Thank you so much for today. I really enjoyed myself."

"Anytime, dear lady."

"I'll see you to your car." She didn't acknowledge that Jayson had stood as well. She hoped that if she ignored him, he'd stay behind. When she opened the front door, she turned to see Jayson standing near the staircase, hands on his hips with a look of frustration etched in his features. *What is his problem?*

Kevin led the way to his car and she gave him a hug once they reached the driver's side. "I really do appreciate all your help, Kevin."

He raised the back of her hand to his lips, briefly brushing them across her skin. "Always happy to help a lady in need."

"There you go again."

"What? I'm simply being a gentleman."

"Yes, you are. It's an odd experience for me. I only

know a couple of men I'd truly call chivalrous."

"I hope you now consider me among them."

She laughed. "Indeed, I do."

Kevin opened the car door and lowered himself into the seat. Before shutting the door, he looked up at her one last time. "Lindsey, keep that guy on his toes." He looked back at the house. "Don't take any crap."

"I don't intend to. I have the impression something is up with you two. What am I missing?"

"Nothing at the moment. Just two guys being guys. I simply want to be sure he's not being a pain in your ass."

She shook her head. "Oh, believe me, that won't be an issue. Besides, I can give as good as I get, so he'd better watch out if he crosses me."

Kevin laughed. "Fantastic. Please allow me a ring side seat should it come to that." He closed the door, started the car, and waved at her one last time as he drove away.

She watched him leave, then turned back to enter the house. Jayson had seated himself on the porch swing near the front door. *Damn! How does he keep sneaking up on me?* Her irritation was gaining momentum.

He crossed one leg over the other and watched her climb the steps to the porch. "So, that's your new *friend*." He made the word friend sound like something sinister.

"Yes. He's been incredibly helpful, and I enjoy his company."

"If you like that type."

"*That* type?" He was starting to piss her off. "If you mean a complete gentleman with a great sense of humor, then yes. I very much like *that* type."

He blew out a breath and ran a hand through his neatly-combed hair. "Sorry, I wasn't meaning to imply anything, I just … I guess I'm a little worried about you. I'm afraid he's making promises he can't keep."

She narrowed her eyes at him. "You mean the Jackson King interview."

He nodded.

"Why on Earth would he do that? What could he possibly gain from lying to me?"

"Do I really have to spell it out? Men lie, Lindsey. Some will say anything to get a woman in bed. With this King thing, he might as well be promising you the moon. He can't deliver."

"Oh, really? And how do you know this?" Her voice pitched an octave to match her rising temper.

"Everyone knows the guy won't do personal interviews. It's a rule he never breaks."

She crossed her arms in front her and raised her eyebrows in inquiry. "Do you know Mr. King?"

He stood. "That's not the point here. He's taking advantage of you. I just want you to be careful." He turned his back to her and entered the house.

"Wait a minute!" She pursued him all the way to the stairs.

"Thank you for the meal; it was wonderful. I know you didn't have to invite me, so I appreciate it." He took two steps up before turning around. "Please leave the dishes. I'll see to them after I've worked a little more. You shouldn't have to cook *and* clean." Without another word, he climbed the remaining stairs and entered his living space.

She stood at the base of the steps and stared up into the darkness of the upper floor. Jayson was easily one of the most confusing men she'd ever met. She was contemplating his waffling temperament when her thoughts were interrupted by her cell phone.

Lindsey walked to the kitchen counter and pulled her phone from her purse. The text icon indicated she had one new message. She opened it to find Shawn had resumed his pursuit of reconciling with her. She had no interest in speaking to him, despite his pleading to give him another chance. She quickly typed back, "Go to hell" then turned her phone off for the evening.

Jayson sat on the edge of his bed and closed his eyes. "What the hell am I doing?" he groaned as he replayed the evening. He had no business going down there and interrupting her date. *Of all the people she had to spend time with, why did it have to be Kevin?* It's like fate was somehow conspiring against him.

His cell phone rang, and without looking at the caller ID he knew who it was.

"Hello."

"Obviously you're thrilled to hear from me," came Kevin's sarcastic reply from the other end.

"Listen, I had no idea she was having dinner with *you*. I was concerned it was some creeper, so I thought I'd better check it out."

"Sure. Sizing up the competition?"

"Not at all. Just making sure she's safe."

"Keep telling yourself that. In the meantime, explain to me why she doesn't know who she's living with."

"It's a misunderstanding. One I'll clear up soon. She won't be staying much longer anyway, so it really doesn't matter."

"What do you know about her plans? Did she say she was leaving?" Kevin's voice held a hint of alarm.

"No, but when she doesn't get that interview, she'll have to return home and get back to her normal life."

"Wow. You really are a jackass." Kevin's voice held a tinge of disbelief.

"I'm just a guy trying to get his work done. You know damn well that I came here for peace and a disturbance-free environment."

"So, you are still sticking to your stupid no personal interviews rule? Even for someone as wonderful as Lindsey?"

"I'm not a horrible person because I don't want to be in the limelight, Kevin. And thanks for making me sound like a dickbag when you described me by the way."

"You are a dickbag. I have to work with you—I should know."

"Dammit, I should have refused to work with you when I had the chance."

"Hey, you keep this anti-publicity crap up and you might get your wish sooner than later. We need you to put in some one-on-one with the public. Book signings and interviews are part of the job, man. Being accessible helps sell books. I honestly don't know why we've let you get away with it this long."

"There won't *be* another book if I can't get people to leave me alone!"

"Maybe you should concentrate on that then, instead of forcing your way into Lindsey's dates."

"Ha! So it was a date!" barked Jayson.

"Not that it's any of your business." Kevin sighed. "Listen, I'm not backing off. Give her the interview. Tell her the truth."

"So I'm just supposed to march downstairs and say, 'Hey, Lindsey, my last name isn't actually Walsh. I'm not Aidan's brother. I'm Jayson Conway and I write under the pen name of Jackson King."

"Something like that. And then tell her you'll do the interview."

"What do you get out of this, Kevin? Why do you care so damn much? If I was going to give an exclusive to anyone, shouldn't it be one of the national publications that have been pestering me for months?"

"Eventually, yes. But give this one to Lindsey. The angle is great, and I know she'll do a great job with it."

"And then what? You get to play the hero and she falls willingly into your arms? I believe this is called a conflict of interest."

"Go to hell, Jayson, right after you grant her the interview."

The line went dead, and Jayson frowned. His policy stood—no personal interviews. Especially if it would help Kevin get into Lindsey's good graces. It wasn't anything against her. She was great, even if she did feel like his writing was, as she said, a little cliché. Despite his efforts, he happened to agree with her somewhat. It was why he'd decided on a change of scenery. He'd hoped the location and solitude would reawaken his muse and get his imagination flowing into areas a little riskier, or original. It had started to work, too, and then distractions disguised as a gorgeous, funny, intelligent woman came barging in wearing a bikini. And she threw things at him. He was pretty sure that paperweight she hit him with knocked all his ability to reason from his body.

He needed to clear his mind of her, and the best way he knew to attempt that was through writing. It was time to get back to work.

Lindsey walked along the beach toward the house, enjoying the sunrise as she tried to calm her frazzled nerves. Her concern over the interview was getting the better of her, despite Kevin's assurance that he'd work it out. It'd been two days since she'd heard from him, and time was running out. All her calls went to his voicemail. She worried that she'd done something wrong.

Then there was Shawn. He seemed to think the two weeks he'd invested in her, as he so gracefully put it, earned him her undying attention. For her, it was validation that breaking up with him and been the right move. Unfortunately, he'd been texting and calling at least once every day. She'd put his number on block, but that only seemed to incense him further, and he started using other numbers to harass her. If she'd been home, she would have probably been a little concerned for her safety. Shawn seemed to be on the edge, and she didn't need that complication in her life. Thankfully, he had no idea where she was.

Her mind wandered to Jayson. She hadn't seen or heard from him since the awkward dinner. She couldn't help but think that the silence with both men had to be connected. She felt certain something had happened between them and she had missed it.

When she reached the back deck, she wiped the sand from her feet and went inside. On the counter sat a bag of donuts and a letter addressed to her.

Lindsey,

I apologize once again for intruding on your date the other night. I had no business prying into your personal affairs. I hope you'll accept these donuts as a peace offering. I ventured out early this morning to get them for you. I'm sure you understand what an undertaking that was for me, considering I tend to be a troll before I get my coffee.

If you have a few moments later today, there is something we need to discuss. Perhaps over lunch? My treat.

Jayson

Something to discuss? She thought that sounded ominous. Lindsey had no idea what they needed to talk about, unless it had something to do with Kevin's silence. She was more worried than ever. She looked down at the letter and chewed on her bottom lip.

"I hope you like chocolate."

She spun around at hearing Jayson's voice directly behind her. *Damn him and his quiet footsteps! Was the man raised by ninjas?*

"Chocolate?" She looked up into his eyes, noticing that the blue in them seemed darker and deeper than she remembered.

He nodded in the direction of the bag behind her. "For the donuts. I wasn't sure what you'd like, but I didn't think I could go wrong with chocolate. Everyone likes chocolate, right?"

"Right." She was still staring up into his face, and repeating words like some idiotic parrot.

"I didn't expect to see you so early, or I'd have just asked you to lunch in person."

She blinked trying to break the pull to him that she felt in that moment. "Oh. That's fine. No problem." She wanted to back away from him and give herself some breathing room, but the counter kept her rooted to the spot.

"So, will you?" His eyes searched her face.

She had to command her brain to function. What did he want her to do? He was too close for comfort. She chided herself. *C'mon girl, snap out of it. You are Lindsey-freaking-Sparks—you don't get flustered over any man.*

"Lindsey, are you okay?" His voice was full of concern.

"Yes, yes, I'm fine." She took a steadying breath. "Lunch? Sure, sounds good."

He knitted his brows together. "Are you sure you're okay?"

"I'm sure. Still waking up, I guess."

He smiled. "Okay, so we'll leave around 11:30."

She nodded.

"Great." He gestured to the stairs. "I guess I'll get back to work. See you in a few hours."

He retreated to his workspace, and she concentrated on making coffee and enjoying her donuts. Her cell phone rang as she poured her second cup.

"Lindsey Sparks speaking."

"Lindsey, it's Kevin. Sorry I've missed your calls. It's been a crazy couple of days. I was called in to deal with a problem at work. I had to go to New York, and it's been a mess."

"Not a problem at all. I understand. Are you back in Florida?"

"No, but I will be later today. I'd like to see you when I get back."

"Oh, sure. That'd be lovely." She winced, knowing she sounded less than enthusiastic.

"Unless you have other plans?" Kevin sounded unsure of himself.

"No, not at all. I'm just distracted. I've been here almost a week and I've gotten nowhere. I'm feeling a little lost, to be honest."

"I'm still working on Jackson, so don't give up there. I had a meeting about him while I was in New York. I think things will be turning around for you very soon."

"Oh, my. Well, thank you for the effort, no matter the outcome." She sincerely appreciated how hard he was working on her behalf.

"I've gotta run, but I'll call you when my plane lands. I can fill you in on things then."

She smiled, hoping the action would make her voice sound cheerful. "I look forward to it."

"Me too, Lindsey. Goodbye for now."

"Bye, Kevin."

She put down her phone and mentally reviewed her interview questions for Jackson King. She had finished his current best seller the night before and had new questions to add to her list. She was still a little nervous, but maybe it was going to work out after all. First, she needed to find out what Jayson was up to. Her gut told her she might not like what she was going to hear. No good news ever started with the words "there is something we need to discuss".

Chapter Eight

JAYSON PACED THE small living area between the kitchen and the back door. He was nervous, and he hated it. Lindsey had agreed to have lunch with him, and he planned to admit that he wasn't a Walsh. Honesty was an important trait to him, yet he'd been lying to her since he learned about her mistaking his identity. Despite being a distraction of epic proportions, she was starting to grow on him. He hoped they could be real friends when it was all said and done.

He thought back to their conversation earlier that

morning. She seemed a little off, and to be honest, so was he. Every time he looked into her green eyes he found himself drowning in emotions he couldn't understand. Those feelings ranged from hating her very presence to wanting to press her against the counter and kiss her senseless. When she was near, his whole world felt as if it was tilting off its axis.

Lindsey opened her bedroom door and stepped out into the living room. She was wearing a white sleeveless dress with straps that crossed in the back, exposing a good portion of her back. Her hair was piled on top of her head in a bun, with several tendrils hanging loose around her face. He took in the woman before him and forgot how to breathe.

"Is this okay? I don't know where we are having lunch, so I wasn't sure what to wear." She sounded self-conscious.

He nodded, not trusting himself to speak.

"Great. Should we go then?"

He cleared his throat. "Absolutely, I'm starved. I hope you like seafood." He led the way to the front door.

"I do." She grinned. "It's probably my favorite cuisine."

"Then you'll love this place. Best little secret on the island."

He walked to a small blue convertible sitting in the driveway and opened the passenger door for her.

Surprise was evident in her expression. "Whose is this?"

"It's mine. I don't use it much on the island since I

prefer my motorcycle, but I can't properly treat a lady to lunch and expect her to hop on the back of my bike."

She smirked and an adventurous gleam entered her eyes. "Oh, I don't know. Depends on the lady I think. Sounds kinda fun to me." She lowered herself into the soft leather seats and buckled up.

The image of Lindsey straddling the motorcycle seat in her dress, her body forming against him as he drove down the seacoast was vivid in his mind. He fought to push it away, but that was a lost cause.

He hopped over the door and settled into his own seat. The engine purred to life as he pulled out of the drive. He purposely took the back roads to allow them to move slower and enjoy the scenery. To avoid the eventual awkward silence, he reached for the radio.

"Do you have a music preference?"

She shrugged. "Not really. I pretty much like it all."

He thought back to the time he caught her singing and winced. *Maybe music isn't a great idea.* "Mind if I ask you some questions?"

She gave him a sidelong look. "I suppose."

"Have you always wanted to be a writer?" *Nice, idiot. Bring up the very subject you aren't ready tackle yet.*

"I have. When I was little girl I used to make up all these crazy stories and entertain my parents with them."

"They must be very proud."

"My dad is, in some ways. Obviously, he'd be happier if I was financially secure, but I keep reminding him, and myself, that it will happen in time. I just have to keep at it."

"I agree."

She shifted in her seat. "What about you? Have you always wanted to be a sculptor?"

Her words were like a punch in the gut. How did he answer that without making things worse? He took a moment to think about it. "I wasn't sure what I wanted to do when I grew up." At least that was the truth. Most of the time his biggest aspiration was to survive long enough to actually become an adult.

"You probably wanted to be superhero. Admit it. You wanted to be Superman." She laughed as she teased him.

"No." He quipped, "I wanted to be Thor. No real guy wanted to grow up wearing tights with his underwear over them."

She laughed again, and he noted how much he enjoyed the sound. He turned into a small gravel lot and parked near a colorful building with the words *Sea Shack* painted over the door.

"Is this it? That didn't take long at all."

"This is a fantastic little place I found a couple of weeks ago. I stumbled upon it while looking for a bookstore I'd heard about. I loved it so much I've been coming back at least once a week."

"Sounds great!"

After exiting his side of the vehicle, he opened the car door for her and held out his hand. She accepted his help, and he relished the warmth of her fingers wrapped around his. He was hesitant to let her go, but he shook off the silly idea of holding her hand and instead gestured for her to go ahead. "Ladies first."

"Really? I expected something more like 'age before beauty.'"

"Well, I didn't want to mention it, but now that you've brought it up …" he teased.

She rolled her eyes and chuckled. "I walked right into that one."

His grin was wide. "Yes, you did." Jayson opened the door for her and she entered the air-conditioned restaurant. The entire building was decorated in a tropical theme. A young man named Alex rushed to seat them and led them to a small table near the window that overlooked the water.

"Can I get you something to drink?" Alex asked, pen poised over his order pad.

"Do you have peach tea?" Lindsey asked.

"Yes, ma'am." His grin was wide, and Jayson thought he caught a hint of bashfulness in the kid.

"That sounds good. I'll have one too." He gave the boy a reassuring smile.

"Awesome. I'll be right back." Alex hurried away to get their beverages while they looked over the menu.

Jayson directed his gaze at Lindsey. "I highly recommend the catch of the day or the crab legs. Both have been phenomenal every time I order them."

"I'll try the catch of the day. I feel like being adventurous today."

"You won't regret it." He looked back at his menu and fought the urge to ask her what other adventures she'd like to get into after lunch. He needed to keep his mind on his mission—prove to her he's a decent guy and explain the mix up about his identity.

She must have picked up on his apprehension. "So, what is this topic we need to discuss?" Her smile wavered, and he could tell she was nervous as well.

Alex appeared with their drinks and carefully placed each one in front of them. "Are you ready to order?"

Lindsey nodded at Jayson, and he answered for them both. "Yes, we'll each have the catch of the day."

"Excellent choice, sir!" Alex's enthusiasm was refreshing, and he caught himself smiling at the kid as he once again rushed to the kitchen to place the order. He made a mental note to give him a big tip when they leave.

Jayson took a big gulp of his tea and resolved to face the situation head on and get it over with. "Lindsey, the reason I wanted to talk to you …" He hesitated, trying to find the right words.

A small elderly woman approached the table with a huge smile and open arms. "Ah! Mr. Conway! It's so very good to see you again! And you brought a lovely friend!"

He returned her smile, but quickly realized she'd used his real name, and he shot a glance at Lindsey. As he expected, she was still smiling, but her eyes gave away her confusion. She looked at him and back to the woman.

"Mrs. Temple, it's a pleasure to see you again."

"Is my grandson, Alex, taking good care of you? This is his first job, and he's a little nervous."

Lindsey spoke up. "He's doing a superb job. I would never have guessed he was new."

Mrs. Temple beamed proudly. "You are too kind, Miss! But I will tell him you said so." She placed weathered fingers on Jayson's arm. "Such a nice lady friend you have there, Mr. Conway. Don't let this one get away!" She winked at him and quickly walked away to answer a ringing phone.

"Jayson, why was she calling you Mr. Conway?" Suspicion laced her voice.

His throat constricted a little and again he fought for the right words to explain. *Why am I being such a coward? If she gets mad, she gets mad. Nothing changes if she hates me.* But even as he thought it, he knew it wasn't true. Something was different, and he was afraid to find out what that something was.

"Jayson, explain please." She crossed her arms and waited.

"You remember the day you arrived and the misunderstanding about the house?"

She nodded.

"Well, you assumed I was Jay Walsh, but that's not exactly true."

"Not exactly?" Her voice rose slightly in volume.

He looked around at the few other patrons in the restaurant to see if they were watching. No one was paying attention so far. "So here's what happened. My name is Jayson Conway. I rented the house from Simon Jay Walsh, but you know Aidan's brother as Jay."

The shocked expression she wore told him volumes. She was going to slap him. He braced himself for a blow that never came.

"You lied to me?" To his surprise, she sounded more hurt than angry.

"I promise I didn't set out to deceive you. It was just a misunderstanding."

She put up a hand to stop him. "One that you continued to perpetuate."

"No, it wasn't like that. I was trying to save you from discomfort or embarrassment."

"By letting me believe you were someone you aren't? Do you have any idea how uncomfortable and embarrassed I am right now? I feel like a total fool! You have an odd sense of courtesy. Wasn't it you that said you value honesty above all else?" He could tell she was struggling to keep her volume at a level that wouldn't attract attention.

When he'd decided to let her believe he was a Walsh, he hadn't considered how she'd feel once she learned the truth. He felt guilty that his biggest concern had been how she'd react to the news, instead of caring how she'd feel about herself. Not that it was her fault.

"Lindsey, it was an honest mistake."

She stood up and her chair teetered before falling to the tile floor and causing a loud echo throughout the small building. "Honest? Don't you dare talk to me about honesty!" She stormed past him and out of the restaurant. Jayson hurried to catch up. As he stood, his foot caught on the table leg and he'd only taken one step before he tripped himself.

He went face first into the table next to theirs. By instinct, he put his hands out to catch himself, but all he managed to do was hit a bowl full of clam chowder. The bowl seemed to move in slow motion as it rose in the air and spun once before dumping the entirety of its contents over his head and landing on the floor with a clatter. The woman eating the chowder was pushed back in her seat as far as she could get, screaming as if she were being attacked.

An elderly man at the other end of the room reacted to the scream by clutching his chest, causing the lady with him to begin shouting for someone to call 911.

A toddler jumped up and down in the booth across from them and shouted "Fries! Fries!" while shoving the food item up his nose. His mother frantically tried to calm him down while rocking her crying newborn.

Alex ran out to see what all the commotion was and slipped in the clam chowder that had made it to the floor, sending the kid sprawling across the tile on this back.

Mrs. Temple cautiously entered the dining area from the kitchen and surveyed the disaster before her. "What in heaven's name happened here?"

Jayson got to his feet and looked around. He was covered in soup, Lindsey was gone, and everyone in the room was shooting him a dirty look. Even the toddler seemed to be giving him the stink eye, and did he just hear the little tike growl?

"I'm so sorry, Mrs. Temple. I'm sorry everyone. I tripped. I'll pay for everyone's lunch."

That seemed to appease the other diners, and they cautiously went back to their meals. The elderly man was breathing heavy but assured the woman with him he was fine. Jayson pulled out his credit card and took it to Mrs. Temple.

"Please, let me pay for all the trouble."

She shook her head. "Don't worry about the mess. I'll let you know how much the meals are. For now, go get your lady before it's too late to patch things up."

He gave her a grateful smile and quickly made his way to the door. As he passed the toddler, the little guy held out a French fry that Jayson was sure had been up the boy's nose. "No thank you," he said as kindly as he could while he rushed out to the parking lot.

Lindsey was gone. He could only assume she'd started walking back home. He brushed off the chunks of soup still clinging to his face and hair, thankful that the soup was only warm and not fresh off the stove. He jumped into his car and sped down the street toward the house. He didn't see her and wondered how she'd gotten so far, so fast. He made a left turn, and within a minute he was behind Lindsey. He pulled alongside her and slowed down.

"Lindsey, I'm sorry. Please, get in the car. Let me drive you back."

She sighed and kept walking, pretending he wasn't there.

"Lindsey, c'mon. Talk to me."

She whirled on him, looking ready to knock him down a few pegs, but she stopped when she saw what a mess he was. "What happened to you?"

He stopped the car. "Soup."

"Soup?"

"I tripped and ended up with soup all over me. Huge domino effect in the restaurant, yadda, yadda, yadda.

Now, will you get in the car, please?" He was trying to be patient, but his pride could only take so much humiliation in such a short time.

She started laughing. At first, it was small giggles that she fought to keep inside. Soon, they were all out belly laughs that had her wiping tears from her eyes. She leaned on the car for support while she caught her breath.

"Great," Jayson said. "Do you feel better now? I'd really like to get home. This chowder smells, and I'm pretty sure it's creeping in to places it doesn't belong." He wiggled as he felt a little spot he'd missed slide down his back.

She didn't say a word as she climbed into the passenger seat. She pressed her lips together in a smirk but kept her laughter under wraps. Jayson drove them home and opened the door for her.

Lindsey entered the house and put her purse on the counter. Her cell chimed, and she groaned. Jayson glanced over at her phone as he walked by and couldn't help but see the very intimate image she'd been sent.

His eyebrows rose in surprise. "You enjoy sexting?"

She turned back to him and quickly grabbed her phone. She looked at her phone and muttered "Dammit! Why won't he leave me alone?"

Jayson frowned. "Is someone bothering you?"

"Yes. No. I … I got it covered. Don't worry about it." Her annoyance was evident in every syllable.

"If you need me to talk to the guy, I will."

"No, thank you. I don't need anything from you." He had hoped her anger had died down after her laugh over the soup, but he knew that was too good to be true.

"Listen, I thought—"

She interrupted him. "You thought I was a hysterical woman who couldn't handle the truth. If you'd have told me right away, I would have been much calmer over the situation. But I *thought* we were beginning to be friends. I *thought* you could be trusted. Now, I'm not so sure."

She grabbed her purse and cell phone, walking away from him swiftly.

He followed her. "I can be trusted. This isn't *that* big a deal."

She entered her bedroom and turned to look him in the eye. "If you can't see why this is a problem, then you're worse than I thought." She slammed the door in his face.

Chapter Nine

LINDSEY SAT ON her bed and cried angry tears. She knew she was probably being a tad irrational, after all, she's the one who'd made the assumption that Jayson was Jay. And in all honesty, her reaction surprised even her. *What was it about Jayson that caused such an extreme emotional response?* Sometimes she liked him; other times she hated him. Whatever the source of her feelings, she needed to get a grip. In a few short days, she'd be on a flight back home, and Jayson would be a memory.

She sighed loudly and reached for a tissue on the

nightstand. A knock on the door made her jump. She frowned and moved to open it.

"Listen, I don't really want to talk to you right now," she snapped.

A surprised Kevin stood in front of her. "You don't?"

"Oh, Kevin! So sorry. I thought … you were someone else." She didn't want to get into it with him, so the less said the better.

"Are you okay? You've been crying. What happened?"

She shook her head and gestured for them to sit on the sofas in the living room. "It's nothing. I'm over it. When did you get back?"

He sat next to her. "I landed and drove straight here from the airport. No one answered the door, but it was unlocked so I let myself in. I hope that's okay."

She nodded as she wiped her nose once more. "Of course, but I thought you were going to call?"

His brows drew together. "I was too excited and wanted to tell you in person." He paused. "Lindsey, I want you to know you can confide in me. If you ever need to talk, I'm here."

She patted him on the arm. "Thank you. That's very kind."

He smiled and leaned closer. "I'm available anytime you need me."

"I'll keep that in mind." She forced a cheerful expression, although she was far from it.

Kevin took one of her hands in his. "I think I have some news that will cheer you up."

"Oh?" She looked at his smile, and a small twinge of

hope fluttered in her chest.

"Yes. I'm setting up that interview for you. I have to work out a couple of details, but I promise you will be meeting Jackson King within the next few days."

"Really?" She squeezed his hand. "You really got him to agree?"

"You're getting the exclusive. No one else will be granted this privileged for quite some time."

She clapped her hands over her mouth and let out a little squeal. He laughed, and she wrapped her arms around him in a big hug. He returned the hug, but held on to her tightly, not letting go when she loosened her grip. Slowly, she pulled away.

Kevin reached up and tucked a stray curl behind her ear. "Lindsey, I'm so happy I met you. I hope you enjoy my company as well."

She nodded. "I do."

"Would you like to have dinner tonight?"

"Sure. What would you like me to make?"

He shook his head. "No, I want to take you out … On a real date, if you'll let me."

"Oh. You're asking me out?"

"I am."

She'd considered him dating material—he lined up perfectly with her list of attributes she was looking for. She should accept and be thankful he was interested in her, but the prospect of actually dating him didn't excite her like it should. Regardless, she thought it was only fair to give him a shot. The idea of saying no since he'd secured an interview sent a ripple of guilt through her. In the back of her mind, she heard Jayson's nagging voice, warning her about lying men and their expectations. *Huh! He'd know all about that, now wouldn't he?* She pushed down the bitter thoughts that had crept back to the surface.

"Lindsey?"

She blinked, realizing Kevin was still waiting on an answer. "Oh, sorry." She took a deep breath. "Yes, I'd be happy to go out with you tonight." She hoped she wasn't making a big mistake.

Kevin beamed at her. "Wonderful! I promise we'll have a great time. I'll pick you up at six, okay?"

Her smile was a little forced, but she kept it in place. "Perfect."

He stood and she followed, both walking to the front door.

"See you tonight." Kevin winked at her and then jogged down the few steps that led to the pathway and his car.

Lindsey closed the door and leaned against it, exhaling a deep, calming breath. She was emotionally drained and physically exhausted. The stress of the much-needed interview, as well as her confused and conflicted feelings about her house-mate, had taken its toll. She needed a nap.

Lindsey rolled over and looked at the clock. She'd slept for almost two hours. Sitting up, she stretched and realized she was feeling a good deal better. What she really needed was to soak in a hot bath and let the water work its magic on what was left of her tension.

She strolled into the bathroom and smiled at the huge clawfoot tub that sat in one corner of the room. She turned the water on and adjusted the temperature to what Whitney had once deemed "melt your skin" hot. She chuckled thinking of her best friend and made a mental note to call her soon. Once the tub was full, she slipped out of her clothes and into the hot water, submerging herself up to her neck. Lindsey leaned her head back and sighed in utter bliss. She really missed soaking in the bathtub. Her tiny apartment only had a shower and the water pressure sucked. *This is a luxury.*

She closed her eyes and let the world slip away, trying to clear her mind of anything and everything. The house was completely quiet, and she was enjoying the silence more than she could have ever imagined.

Then she heard something.

She couldn't place it, but whatever it was, it was in the bathroom with her. She peeked over the edge of the tub just in time to see a flash of something long slither behind the toilet. She screamed.

Mere moments later, Jayson came bursting through the door.

"What? What happened?" He looked around frantically, but froze when he noticed she was in the bathtub. After a moment of obvious struggle, his eyes met hers.

She screamed again and tried to hide herself as much as possible.

He turned his back to her. "Why are you screaming, woman?"

She pointed past him to the area where the toilet and sink were located. "I saw something. A snake! It went behind the toilet I think!" She hated the panic in her voice. There wasn't much that scared Lindsey, but she was terrified of snakes.

He cautiously approached the area, grabbing her towel off the rack as he squatted down to get a better look. Lindsey stayed hunkered down behind the side of the bathtub and watched with wide eyes as Jayson searched for the creature.

He caught movement out of the corner of his eye and turned his head just in time to see a tail disappear behind a small space between the wall and the sink. It was heading toward Lindsey.

"Where is it?" she whispered in impatience.

Jayson turned to look at her and she sunk lower in the tub. "It's behind the sink. And you don't need to whisper. I don't think it cares what we say or how loud we say it."

She narrowed her eyes at him. "Laugh it up, funny boy."

"What? You're the one whispering like we have some kind of secret we can't let it hear."

"Keep talking, and I'll start throwing soap and shampoo bottles at you."

Jayson stood, still holding her towel. "Fine. I'll leave you to enjoy your bath and your snake." His smile was bordering on evil. At that moment, she was sure he was the devil.

"*No*," she shouted and reached out for him. "Don't leave me!"

That movement allowed him to see more of her chest that she'd wanted him to. His smile faded, and he cleared his throat. He walked toward her.

"What are you doing? Don't come any closer!"

He took another step.

"Jayson! Stop!"

And another step.

"Damn you! Where is your decency?" she pleaded as he stood by the edge of the tub. She used a washcloth and her hands to attempt to cover herself as he looked down at her.

He put a finger to his lips. "Shhh."

Her mouth flew open in shock. "Did you just shush me?"

He leaned down and she looked up at the intensity and concentration in his eyes. *He's going to kiss me. Do I want that? Do I want what that could lead to in this moment?* She closed her eyes.

Jayson suddenly lunged forward with the towel in hand and slammed it against the wall next to her. "Got it!"

She opened her eyes to see him leaned over her and the tub, his hands held the towel tightly against the wall and a trapped lump wriggled underneath. She froze.

He carefully placed one hand over the lump and grabbed it, wrapping it up in the towel. Lindsey thought she'd faint. The very idea of him holding a snake made her queasy.

He stepped back and peeked inside the towel, making sure he had the animal secure.

"Are you a lunatic? Why are you holding that thing? Get rid of it!"

He smirked. "It's not a snake, it's a lizard. They're pretty common around here."

She frowned. "Really? It's not dangerous, is it?"

He shook his head. "Not at all."

He stepped closer to show her and she put up her hand.

"No, thank you. I don't need to see it. I believe you."

"Well, glad to know I can be trusted on something."

She thought she heard anger in his voice, or maybe a tinge of hurt? Once again, her thoughts and emotions were scrambling her brain.

"Can we talk about this later? I'd like to get out." She smiled, hoping he'd retreat peacefully.

He nodded. "Sure. We'll talk when you've dressed."

He stepped out of the room, and she slowly stood.

He poked his head back around the door. "Oh, I have your …" the words died on his lips as he saw Lindsey in all her naked glory "…towel." He managed to finish his sentence a second later.

She screamed, "Jayson!" and threw a bar of soap at him. He ducked back out as the soap hit the door. A different towel came flying through the doorway and she heard him say, "There ya go. A lizard-less towel."

"Thank you," she ground out between clenched teeth.

"No, thank you." He chuckled. "It's not even Wednesday."

Jayson sat on the sofa waiting for Lindsey to exit her bedroom. *She's going to kill me. She's going to find something sharp and stab me with it a million times.* He smiled. *Totally worth it.*

The door opened, and she stepped out. He shot up, ready to defend himself from whatever she'd probably throw at him. He was surprised to see her dressed to the nines in a short black dress with silver accents, black heels, and her hair was piled up on top of her head, exposing her neck. He found himself staring at the spot where her neck and shoulder met. He loved that spot on a woman. He loved that spot on her. *Down, boy! You can't think about her like that!*

She noticed him staring and blushed. He assumed she was embarrassed because he'd seen her naked earlier. He really hadn't meant for that to happen, and he planned to apologize, although he couldn't be completely sorry, if he were honest with himself.

"Lindsey, I'm sorry for earlier."

She shook her head. "No, I'm sorry. You were helping me, and I was just being a hag. Thank you for getting rid of the lizard … and the clean towel."

He bowed. "Happy to be at your service."

She chuckled and rolled her eyes.

"I absolutely owe you an apology about lunch," he said. "My intention was to tell you the truth about myself, but it didn't quite happen the way I'd planned."

"It's okay. The mistake was mine to begin with."

"True, but I could have corrected you, and I didn't." He hoped she sincerely saw how much he regretted his lack of action.

"No, you didn't." She shot him a look of annoyance.

"Can I make it up to you? I make a mean grilled cheese sandwich."

"Thanks, but I have a date with Kevin."

He frowned.

"What now?" she asked.

"I don't think you should date him."

She raised an eyebrow. "Good thing you don't have a say in it then."

"I don't trust him."

"You don't need to. But I do, and that's all that matters here. Don't you have some kind of work to do?" She raised an eyebrow at him.

He threw his hands up in the air in surrender. "Fine. Don't say I didn't warn you." Then he stomped up the stairs and entered his room, slamming the door behind him.

He sat at his desk and stared at his laptop, letting his mind wander back to the maddening woman downstairs. *Why is she dead set on being with Kevin?* Jayson had only known him for the last couple of months since he was new to the publisher, and while they got along okay in their working relationship, he didn't care for Kevin personally. Something about the man always rubbed him the wrong way.

He was moving in on Lindsey and that really pissed him off. She was a handful, but overall seemed to be a nice woman. He knew she could do better. *Like who? You?* The thought popped into his head in an instant, and he was floored by it. Had he thought about her sexually? Sure, he's only human, after all, and she's a gorgeous woman. Since he'd seen even more of her, he was sure those thoughts wouldn't go away anytime soon. Did he want more than that? He'd never considered it. Work was his mistress, and no woman would ever put up with the life he led for long. She deserved better than him for sure.

Work. Odd how he hadn't been obsessing over it as much the last couple of days. He was going to miss his deadline again if he wasn't careful. As much as it pained him to admit it, Lindsey was right. He had work to do.

Chapter Ten

LINDSEY WALKED THROUGH her front door just before midnight. She was tired and slightly over-whelmed. Dinner with Kevin was nice. He'd taken her to a cozy little steak house, and then to a movie. It was a perfectly wonderful time. Not a thing she could complain about. At the door, Kevin had kissed her goodnight. It was fine as well, and that bugged the hell out of her. She struggled to get past the fact that while he was cute, a gentleman, and humble, there was zero spark between them. She had hoped the kiss would ignite something, but there wasn't even a flicker on her end.

She kicked off her shoes and carried them to her room. The idea of her comfortable bed and a solid night of sleep sounded wonderful. When she opened her door, she found a letter sitting on her bed. She closed the door, sat down next to the letter, and rubbed her temples. She wasn't sure she wanted to deal with Jayson right then— on paper or otherwise. In the end, curiosity won out.

> *Lindsey,*
>> *I did not tell you my real name,*
>> *Although initially you were to blame.*
>> *I stuck my nose where it shouldn't be,*
>> *And then I made you mad at me.*
>> *It all got worse when I rushed in*
>> *And saw you in your birthday skin.*
>> *So please forgive my lack of tact,*
>> *Sometimes I forget how to act.*
>> *I hope we can get past all I've done wrong,*
>> *If it makes you feel better I'll show you my...*
>> *Gong.*

> *Jayson, who sucks at poetry but hopes it made you smile.*

Lindsey placed a hand over her mouth and closed her eyes. She tried her best not to smile. She really shouldn't. She wanted to stay mad at him. Her eyes drifted back to the worst poem she'd ever read and she couldn't hold it in; the laughter hit before she could stop it. She flung herself back on the bed and looked up at the ceiling. *What is he doing up there? If he doesn't sculpt, what does he do? Is he in bed, possibly thinking of me right now?*

She frowned at that thought. He wasn't the kind of guy she was looking for. He was a loner and pretty full of himself, although he did at least know how to apologize. This mess wasn't completely his fault. She did make assumptions about his identity. She also screamed about the lizard and he came to her rescue, the nudity part couldn't be helped. As for his beef with Kevin, she had no idea what that was about, but it wasn't anything that should concern him. Lindsey didn't think there would be another date anyway. Hopefully, Kevin felt as underwhelmed with their kiss as she did.

She slipped out of her dress and into a loose, oversized t-shirt. She needed to get some rest, but she already knew she wasn't going to sleep right away. Her mind was racing about everything that had happened in the last few days. Grabbing her laptop, she powered it on and decided to send an email to Mr. Clayton with the latest developments. She'd been updating him regularly, and so far, his responses had all been along the lines of "just keep trying." She knew he believed she couldn't do it, which of course made her want to succeed even more.

After she filled him in on Kevin's promise to set up the interview, she hit send and decided she needed a drink. A little wine usually helped her relax, so it was worth a shot. She opened the door a crack to see if Jayson was downstairs. She couldn't see or hear anything, so she decided it was safe to leave her room. She really didn't want to see him just then. Her thoughts were too muddled for a conversation of any kind with him.

Once she reached the kitchen, she searched for a bottle wine, but all she found was whiskey. She'd never had it, but she had friends who loved the stuff. "No time like the present," she muttered as she poured herself a glass. She started with just a sip, and while it burned going down, she found it soothing once it hit. She took another sip and again enjoyed the warm sensation she felt once the harshness wore off. *This will work nicely.* She filled the glass and took it to the deck to enjoy.

The air was cool, but it felt good on her skin. The ocean could be heard, but not seen. Lindsey sipped her drink and leaned back in one of the padded loungers facing the water. She continued to drink as she listened to the waves roll back and forth. As she felt herself start to relax, she closed her eyes and eventually dozed off.

"Lindsey? Are you okay?"

Her eyes fluttered open to see Jayson standing over her. A lock of hair had fallen into his face as he bent down to check on her. She reached up to push it back. "That's cute." She snickered.

"Why are you out here?" He picked up her glass, a small amount of amber liquid was still present in the bottom, and his frown deepened. "Are you drunk?"

She shook her head and it made everything spin. "No! Not at all. I just had a glass of whiskey."

He sat in the chair next to hers. "You don't strike me as a whiskey sort of girl."

She put a finger to her lips. "Shhh! Don't tell anyone

that. I have a reputation to uphold."

He crossed his arms. "Do you now? Well, I promise it will be our little secret. So, again, why are you out here getting drunk?"

She frowned. "I don't know." Her hand went to her temple as she tried to remember. "I think I was confused about stuff."

"Stuff."

She nodded. "Yes, lots of confusing stuff up here." Her finger tapped at the side of her head, and she tried to bring his face into focus. "You aren't wearing a shirt."

"No, I'm not. I was in bed. You aren't wearing pants."

Looking down she noticed her legs were bare and her shirt was hiked up a little exposing her underwear and belly button. "Where did my pants go? Did you take them?" She squinted her eyes at him in suspicion.

Jayson sighed. "No, I didn't. I'm gonna guess that you forgot to put them on."

She giggled. "I did! I forgot my pants. I should get them." She tried to stand up, but the deck kept moving under her feet.

Jayson grabbed her arm and pulled her against him. "Whoa, I don't think you're gonna make it. Let me help."

She nodded, and he attempted the first step. Her legs felt like rubber, and she slid toward the floor. He stopped her from landing on her butt, then put one arm under her legs and lifted her up. She wrapped her arms around his neck and relaxed her head on his chest.

He used his foot to open the door wide enough for them to get through and walked into the living area. He stood there a moment, and she wondered what he was waiting on.

"What are we doing?" she asked in a sleepy voice. She was still very relaxed and Jayson was warm and comfortable.

"I have no damn idea." He sounded a little frustrated.

"I should probably go to bed." She yawned.

"I think you're right." He walked to her bedroom door and again pushed it open with his foot. He carried her to the bed and lowered her to the mattress.

Lindsey didn't let go of him. "Did you mean it?"

Jayson was working to free her hands from his neck. "Mean what?"

She pulled his face close to hers. "Did you mean it when you said you were sorry?"

He looked into her eyes. "I did."

She smirked. "Did you mean the other thing?"

"What other thing?"

"You said you'd show me your gong."

He laughed. "My gong is tiny, so I'm not sure it would impress you much."

Her eyes went wide. "You have a tiny ..." Her eyes traveled down his chest.

"No, *that* isn't tiny. But, I said my gong. It's a little brass-colored object that makes noise when you hit it. It's on my desk, but I can bring it down if you really want to see it."

Lindsey blinked rapidly as she tried to comprehend his words. "You're such a funny smart ass."

"I aim to please."

She frowned. "Did you see it all?"

"It all? You mean did I see all of your body?"

"Yes." She pouted.

"I saw most of it." He gave her a reassuring smile. "But don't worry, I forget stuff all the time, so maybe I'll forget I saw you."

She let go of his neck and relaxed back into the pillow, closing her eyes. "I hope you don't."

"Don't what?"

"Forget me. I don't want you to forget me." Her voice was all but a whisper.

He looked down at her for several minutes. She'd started snoring lightly, and he realized she'd fallen back asleep.

Softly, he said, "Forget you? Hell, I couldn't forget you if my brain was removed from my head."

Jayson woke up in a foul mood. He'd spent most of the night dreaming about Lindsey. In his dream, he'd spent all day with her. They'd been on the beach together, and she had suggested skinny dipping. He quickly shed his clothes, and just as she was about to take her bikini off, Kevin arrived and took her with him. He ran after her, calling her name, but she never looked back. Then he realized he was naked and all the passing cars were honking at him.

He shook off the nightmare. He pulled a shirt over his head and went downstairs to make coffee. He also decided to go over his latest manuscript. He needed to get his mind back on work. Every time he thought he'd escaped her intrusions, something happened to pull him back in. The dream especially irked him. He didn't care if Kevin took Lindsey. They were friends, sort of, and that's all. Jayson seeing her naked didn't change that. Nor did her words as he put her to bed the night before. She was drunk. Drunk people just say random stuff and you can't bank on that.

He poured his coffee and took a grateful sip, then ventured to the living room to go over his work. He'd just finished reading the first chapter when Lindsey's door opened. She looked like hell, and he still thought she was beautiful. A part of him hated her for it. That only made him more irritable. *Why does she have to look so damn amazing all the time?*

She leaned against her door frame and yawned. "Did you get the info on the bus that hit me last night?"

"I'm pretty sure it was a bottle and not a truck." He continued reading and tried not to look at her mostly bare legs.

"Ah, I vaguely remember that bottle. I think I'm better off sticking to wine." She rubbed her forehead.

"There's coffee in the kitchen and aspirin in the cabinet." He didn't look up at her.

"Thanks." She shuffled to the kitchen, and he could hear her rummaging around in the cabinets.

Soon she was back in the living room, her coffee in one hand and the bottle of aspirin in the other. Lindsey sat on the sofa next to him, took a sip, and exhaled a blissful sigh. Her hands twisted at the cap on the medicine, but it wouldn't budge. She tried again and once more it refused to move. She stopped a moment and just frowned at the bottle.

Jayson stuck out his hand. "Give it here. I'll get it."

She passed it to him and he swiftly popped the lid off.

"Thanks." She accepted the bottle and dug out two pills, then downed them with more coffee.

"How … how did I get to my room last night? I don't fully remember. I'm not sure what was a dream and what was reality."

He put down his papers and looked at her. "I carried you. You were drunk and couldn't walk." He couldn't hide a smirk as he said, "Did your date go that bad?"

"No, actually, it was … fine."

"Fine? Your date was fine?" He sat the papers aside and turned to face her.

"Yeah, so?"

"So is that what you want from a relationship? Fine?"

She frowned at him. "What's wrong with fine?"

He shook his head. "I can't discuss this with you." Grabbing his cup, he stood up and went into the kitchen for a refill. *Fine. Who wants to settle for fine? Fine is boring. Fine is sad and pathetic. Fine is for scared people.*

"What's up your ass?" She stood in the kitchen doorway and watched him doctor his coffee in a rushed manner.

"Nothing. I'm—" He almost said fine, but now he hated the word. "Nothing is wrong."

"Okie dokie, weirdo." She turned and walked back

into the living room.

He took his coffee back into the living room, only to see her peeking at a page of his manuscript. *Oh, hell.* "Hey! Get your nose out of my stuff!"

She had the decency to look guilty. "Sorry, I was just wondering what was so interesting earlier. Did you write this?"

He scooped up the papers. "That's none of your business." His tone was harsh and he didn't care. He was frustrated and tired. Both were because of her, even if it wasn't intentional.

She held up her hands. "Fine."

He growled at her use of that word. Again.

Lindsey glanced up at the clock. "Crap! I need to get busy. It looks like I have that interview tonight, and I don't want to show up unprepared. I need make sure I have all I need on King."

Jayson froze. "Hold up! You have an interview with Jackson King? Tonight?"

She nodded. "Yes, Kevin set it up. He has to get back with me, but he was sure tonight would be fine."

Jayson had heard the phrase "seeing red" but had never believed it was literal, until that very moment.

"So, Jackson King actually agreed to give you an exclusive?"

She stopped and bit her lip. "Well, I'm not sure. Kevin made it sound like he agreed, but I don't recall Kevin actually using those words." Worry creased her features. "Surely he did. Why would Kevin say that if it wasn't a done deal?"

Jayson rolled his eyes. "Yes. Why would a man ever lie to a gorgeous woman he's trying to sleep with?" The sarcasm in his statement was thick.

She put her hands on her hips. "What is it with your obsession over Kevin and I having sex?"

He frowned. "I'm not obsessed. I couldn't care less who you knock boots with, but I do feel it's important to warn a lady when I see a scumbag chasing after her."

"Why are you so sure he's a scumbag? What evidence do you have? Show me the proof, and I'll kick him to the curb."

"Just … It's a gut thing. Never mind." He sighed. "I need to get back to work. Have a good day."

"Lord, you're the most confusing man I've ever had the frustration of knowing. Pick a mood and go with it!"

Jayson stopped at the foot of the stairs and turned to face her. He opened his mouth to say something but stopped himself. His jaw clenched as he took a moment to look her over. Then he shook his head, turned, and walked up the stairs.

Chapter Eleven

JAYSON ENTERED HIS room and tossed his manuscript across the room. Picking up his cell, he furiously dialed Kevin's number.

"Kevin Simpson speaking."

The cheerful greeting only irritated Jayson more. "You lying bastard!"

"Hold on, buddy! Don't you call me and start yelling."

"I'm not your damn buddy, and I never will be. Now, you get this through your thick skull—you do not have the authority to set up an interview for me. It's in my contract. I know you guys want me in front of the public, but I have my reasons for saying no. You do not supersede that!"

"Calm yourself, diva. I didn't set up an interview for you."

"Then why does Lindsey say you did?" He could barely contain his anger.

"That's not with you. That's with Jackson King."

"What? What the hell are you talking about?"

Kevin spoke slowly. "I said it's with Jackson King, or at least someone everyone will think is Jackson King."

Jayson used his finger and thumb to massage the bridge of his nose. He was sure he felt a headache coming on. "You're setting up an interview with a fake?"

"Why not? You never intend to take the credit, so why not let someone else have the fame as long as you get the paycheck."

"Are you insane?" He couldn't believe what he was hearing.

"It makes sense. You get the money, we hire a guy to play you in public, and everyone gets what they want. Everyone is happy."

"You are insane. Kevin, there are so many ways that could backfire."

"Possibly, but not likely. I can draw up a contract with a confidentiality clause."

"Hell no. Call it off."

Kevin didn't respond.

"I know you heard me. Call it off now."

"It's either you, or the impostor. Your choice." Kevin

hung up.

Jayson gripped the phone and fought off the impulse to throw it out of the window. He knew Kevin was pushy, but he never realized how unethical the man was until then. He wasn't just lying to the public, he was lying to Lindsey. She was going to interview the wrong man, and he had to put a stop to it. He just needed to figure out how without revealing his secret.

He looked at his phone and released a sad, heavy sigh. *Speaking of secrets, I guess it's time I check in.* He took a deep calming breath as he dialed the number, then he sat on the edge of his bed and braced himself.

"Yeah, what do you want?" came the harsh but familiar voice over the line.

"Hi. I just wanted to check on you. Are you doing okay?" He fought to keep his voice calm.

"I'm fine, boy, no thanks to you."

"Pete, I sent you a check. Did you get it?"

"I got it." The man's voice was resentful and bitter.

"Are your bills all paid for the month then?"

"I guess. I don't know. I gave it to Tabby so she could deal with all that."

Jayson groaned. *Tabby? Who the hell is Tabby? His latest drinking buddy? Hooker? His newest fling?* He never knew with Pete. "Did you call that number I gave you?"

"Dammit, boy! I don't need no therapist or clinic! Stop stickin' your nose where it doesn't belong!"

"Take care, Pete. Talk to you soon." It was Jayson's turn to hang up first.

Jayson had been sending Pete Taggert small amounts

of money to keep him from living on the street, but the man had never appreciated the gesture. With each check, he became increasingly belligerent. Jayson knew he blew most of his money on gambling and booze, staying in a perpetual state of drunkenness. Jayson often reminded himself that it wasn't Pete's fault that he was the way he was. Jayson couldn't allow him to sink any lower than he already had.

He placed the phone on his desk and set to work picking up the loose sheets of his manuscript. Thoughts swirled through his mind like a tornado, picking up ideas and then tossing it aside just as quickly. They landed on Lindsey and lingered. A smile crossed his face as he sat back down at his computer. He had a wonderful idea. His story had just taken an astounding turn.

Lindsey stepped out of her room at precisely five o'clock. She was decked out in her favorite gray silk blouse and black pencil skirt. She placed a diamond stud in one ear then the other as she walked to the front of the house. Her purse was slung over her shoulder and she double checked to assure everything she needed was inside. As she stepped out into the sunlight, she heard a low whistle. Looking toward the sound, she saw Jayson. He was leaning against one of the porch supports and smiling at her with a grin that she could only describe as mischievous. He wore a pair of snug faded jeans and a black button-up shirt, rolled up at the cuffs. His shoes were classic Converse high tops in black. His blond hair seemed messier than usual, yet she couldn't help but feel as if he'd dressed carefully. He made casual look elegant.

"You look beautiful." His appreciate gaze roved over her slowly.

She narrowed her eyes and hesitated before replying, "Thank you." She placed one hand on her hip. "Why do you look like the cat that ate the canary?"

He feigned innocence. "Me? How could you accuse me of such a thing? I happen to think birds are an amazing species. I'd never harm one."

"Whatever," she said with exasperation. "I need to go, so feel free to unleash your chaos on someone else." She stepped past him and down the steps. He followed.

She stopped and turned to face him. "Why are you following me?"

His smile was wide. "Because shoving you out of the way to get to my car would be rude."

She had to bite back the smirk that threatened to break through. *Why do I find this man so annoying one minute and so adorable the next?* "I'd call you a jackass, but I'd hate to insult the jackass."

He clutched his chest. "Ouch! That barb was a direct hit to the heart."

She turned and continued to her car. "Nonsense. You'd have to possess a heart for that to be possible." Reaching her car, she pulled open the door and tossed in her purse.

"Well, now you're just being mean."

"Yeah, that's me. I'm a horrible person. You should

avoid me at all costs." She sat in the driver's seat and closed the door. He knocked on her window and she rolled it down. "What now?"

"Enjoy your evening." He turned and approached his own vehicle.

She sat in silence for a moment, then looked in her rear view mirror. *What was all that about?* Jayson was unusually jovial, and it made her suspicious. Her gut told her he was up to something, although she had no idea what it could be.

Jayson drove away, and moments later she pulled out behind him. As she drove, her thoughts lingered on the argument they'd had earlier in the day about Kevin. He was nice guy, and he seemed to genuinely want to help her. Jayson simply didn't know what he was talking about. He didn't know her or Kevin, so his comments on their relationship were all conjecture. It bugged her that Jayson was so involved. He was the one that insisted they avoid each other during their brief but forced association, yet every time she turned around, he was right there.

She pulled into the parking lot of Kevin's favorite restaurant, The Ivory Room, and turned off the engine. Despite her confidence in her abilities, she was nervous. It wasn't just any interview; it was *the* interview. The one that would finally push her stagnant career forward. It was a bonus that her success would be giving those old goats back home the finger.

Inhaling a deep breath, she got out of the car and strode toward the door with her spine straight and her head held high. She walked with purpose and determination. She was gonna kick ass with the interview. Heaven help anything that got in her way.

Jayson sat at a table in the corner as his eyes scanned the room for familiar faces. He knew Kevin would be arriving any moment with the fake Jackson King by his side. He was curious to see who Kevin had chosen to be the face of their star writer. Jayson also couldn't wait to see this impostor fall flat on his ass during the interview, if it got that far. Even if the guy had done all his homework, it didn't seem plausible that he could pass himself off as someone he wasn't. He'd trip up somewhere, and Jayson was going to sit back and enjoy the show. He hated that Lindsey would be a casualty when it all fell apart, but that was the price she'd have to pay for not trusting him. He rationalized that while she didn't know him well, she should be able to tell that his concerns for her were sincere. Her stubborn pride was getting in the way of her accepting the truth—Kevin was a dishonest assclown.

He scanned the menu once more, not really seeing the options. His mind was alternating between his latest plot twist and the night's potential for disaster. When he looked up, he noticed the hostess was seating Lindsey at a nearby table. Damn! He'd hoped that Kevin and "Fake Jackson" would arrive first so he could confront them. Instead, he'd have to watch and play things by ear.

The waiter stopped by her table and gave her a menu and the wine list, assuring her he'd be back momentarily.

She glanced at the choices before her then scanned the part of the room directly in front of her. He was thankful that she'd been seated with her back to him, so she didn't notice his presence as she looked around. Lindsey seemed confident, but he also picked up a nervousness that was subtle, but present. It was more like a feeling or vibe than an actual physical attribute. It astounded him that he could know her so little, yet so well that small details like that stood out to him. Maybe it was because he was used to studying people and their behaviors for his books. Or it was possibly due to his spending more time with Lindsey than he normally did anyone, at least while working. He found when he was in "the zone", he was hyper-focused on the little things. Oddly, he'd felt less focused and more frustrated by her presence in his life. At the same time, he was getting ideas faster than he could write them down. So much so that he'd recently decided to change a major plot point in his latest work. He had to reluctantly admit that she was at least partially responsible for his newest rush of creativity. It baffled him.

She sipped from her water glass and checked her watch. Kevin was late. Jayson silently hoped that Kevin's asinine plan had fallen through. As much as he'd like to see Kevin's real side exposed, he also didn't want to see Lindsey hurt. She was a pain in his ass and stubborn as a mule, but she certainly had her charms. With that thought, he had to push back images of Lindsey standing in the tub, soapy water running down her naked body. That was not a something he should be lingering on, even if it was one if his favorite memories.

He cleared his mind and watched from behind his menu as Kevin and a handsome young man approached her table. She stood and Kevin gave her an intimate looking hug and peck on the cheek that appeared possessive, even from Jayson's position a few tables away. Anger quickly boiled to the surface, and Jayson had to tamp it back down. *She's not yours, Jayson, you have no right to get mad or interfere.* He looked on as Kevin made introductions, and she shook Fake Jackson's hand. Once they were all seated, Kevin ordered wine and settled in near Lindsey with a smile. His arm rested casually near her hand, as if he were ready to hold it in a moment's notice.

He studied Fake Jackson. He looked like something out of GQ, and it made Jayson cringe. Dark hair, bright-blue eyes, and an athletic physique—he was too perfect. No doubt Kevin felt a male model type would sell more books. The whole situation was becoming more disgusting by the minute. He lowered his menu and glared at the side of Kevin's head. Kevin must have felt the furious vibes Jayson sent his way, because he looked up and stared right into the eyes of the last man he likely wanted to see that night. For a moment, Jayson saw alarm register on his face, but he quickly smoothed his features and tried to ignore the fact that the real Jackson King was only a few tables away.

Once again, the waiter approached and took their orders, then swiftly returned to the kitchen. Jayson was too far away to really hear any of their voices, but it appeared they were simply having dinner and that the interview would be saved until later.

When his waiter finally got around to him, he ordered a light meal and then kept his eyes trained on Kevin. He was determined to make the night as uncomfortable as possible for the lying weasel.

The meal seemed to pass by with little more than light conversation and Kevin's outward show of possession toward Lindsey. He'd touch her often and she'd smile at him each time, although she always pulled away from his touch moments later. Jayson wondered if she was the kind of woman that didn't like public displays of affection. The more he watched their table, the less appetite he had.

Once the dishes were cleared away and coffee was served, Lindsey pulled out a small notebook, pen, and digital recorder. Jayson was dying to get closer and hear the questions she'd prepared. From what he'd gathered, she'd done a lot of research and was going in fully armed. She pointed her pen at Fake Jackson as she spoke, and he smiled graciously as he listened. But after about ten minutes he was starting to look nervous and he kept flicking his glance toward Kevin. An almost imperceptible nod of encouragement was returned, but it seemed to do nothing for the man's unease. Fake Jackson loosened his tie and fidgeted with his spoon as he spoke. *Damn, I wish I could hear them! It looks like it's getting good!*

Determined to end the little charade, Jayson placed money on the table and stood. At the same time, Fake Jackson stood. He loudly stammered, "I'm so sorry. This was a mistake. I just can't." Then he made a hasty exit past the hostess station and out of the door. Kevin frowned and placed an arm around Lindsey in a comforting gesture. She bowed her head a moment, then raised her face to Kevin's and gave him a brave smile. Her posture had slumped a bit, and she no longer had that aura of excitement and nerves that had surrounded her earlier.

Jayson decided to sit back down before she saw him. He found himself angry at not only Kevin, but Fake Jackson. *How could they do this to her?* He knew it was hypocritical, considering he'd just planned on doing the same thing, more or less. But he had a right to be indignant at what they tried to pull off. They were pretending to be him, after all. But Lindsey was an innocent in all of it. She was just trying to do her job. It would have been better to let her go back without the interview than to think she had it and had somehow blown it.

She stood abruptly and spoke in hushed tones, then picked up her things and went outside. Kevin shot a glare Jayson's way, as if he'd had something to do with the poser leaving, paid the check, and followed her outside. Jayson decided his best move was to wait for her at home. He'd figure out what to do about Kevin later.

Chapter Twelve

LINDSEY UNLOCKED THE door to the house and inhaled a deep breath. It was over. She'd failed. She'd been there over a week, and it had taken every day up to that point to secure the interview. *Why did he run out on me? What did I say?* She'd assumed he was a little eccentric or odd, but the way he left was beyond strange. He'd actually seemed sick, and maybe a little scared.

Kevin broke into her thoughts as he followed her inside. "I'm so sorry, Lindsey. I had no idea he'd be so flighty. I'll talk to him again tomorrow."

"It's okay." She shrugged, feeling completely defeated.

Kevin put his hands on her arms and turned her to face him. "Really. It'll be fine. I'll fix it. I promise."

"Please, don't worry about it, Kevin. I don't want to damage any potential future business relationship with Mr. King. Maybe someday he'll be ready. If so, I hope he'll consider me for the interview."

Kevin eyed her cautiously. "You're being very gracious about this. I'd be hopping mad if someone walked out me like that."

"I'm determined and dedicated to my job, but I'm also a realist. Mr. King seems to have some kind of anxiety, and I'm guessing that's why he's turned down interview opportunities in the past. Am I correct?"

Kevin took his time answering, seeming to mull her statement over. "Something like that."

"It's okay. My mother had anxiety. It was crippling. My heart always ached for her. She wanted to do so many things, but the panic just wouldn't allow her out of her comfort zone." Her lips formed a sad smile. "Please tell Mr. King I understand, and I won't push him further, but I'll be more than happy to speak to him again if he decides he's ready."

Kevin looked shocked and a little frustrated. "That's very kind of you, but I don't think it's necessary. I'm sure I can work this out."

"Anxiety isn't something you just decide to get over Kevin. Even with the right meds it can be a living hell at times." Lindsey decided not to mention her own stint with panic attacks as a young girl, and those were nothing compared to her mother's experiences. "I don't want to drive him into a more aggressive attack by being persistent."

"Lindsey …" Kevin began.

She held up a hand. "It really is okay, Kevin. I'll figure something out."

He looked at her intently. "What if … What if he did the interview over email? Would that be acceptable? There's no immediate pressure that way."

She considered the idea. "That might work, but only if Mr. King is one hundred percent on board with it. I don't want to make him uncomfortable in any way. I realize that asking him to share about himself can feel like an intrusion."

Kevin clapped his hands together and smiled. "Fantastic. I'm sure he'll be fine with that compromise. I can get you a photo to go with it. I'm sure he has a usable one somewhere."

She gave him a tired smile. "I'm sure whatever you can come up with will be fine."

He stepped close and reached his arms around her to pull her against him. She tried to step back, but he wouldn't loosen his grip.

"Kevin, I don't think …"

His lips came down hard on hers, and the kiss was almost bruising. She pushed at him, but his grip was firm. When he pulled back, she was furious.

"What the hell, *Kevin*?" She attempted another shove, but he didn't budge.

"Lindsey, please. Don't turn me away. Let me stay

with you tonight." He looked toward the stairs. "Or you can come home with me."

"Listen, Kevin, I like you, but I don't think we're suited for more than friendship."

He frowned. "Why is that? I'm a nice guy. I have looks, charm, money … What more could you want?"

She made a disgusted face and pushed at him again. That time, he let go just a fraction, giving her room to breathe. "Seriously? You think looks, charm, and money are all a woman needs to sleep with a guy? Hell, if I wanted that I could go back to Shawn!"

His frowned deepened. "Who's Shawn?" His grip tightened, and his fingers dug into her arms.

"Ouch! You're hurting me! Let go!" She wriggled to loosen his grasp.

A low menacing voice called out behind her, "She said let go."

It was Jayson. He sounded calm, but the undercurrent was unmistakable. He was furious.

Kevin relaxed his grip and then rubbed her upper arms.

"Stop touching her," Jayson growled.

Lindsey saw her chance to escape, so she quickly moved backward several steps, putting a decent distance between herself and Kevin.

Kevin reached for her. "Lindsey …"

Jayson was between them in a flash. "It's time you went home."

Kevin glared at him. "I think that's something for Lindsey to decide."

From behind Jayson, she said, "Yes, you need to leave."

"If that's what you want," Kevin said in a hushed tone.

He took a few steps toward the door and then turned. "I'll call you tomorrow, Lindsey." When Jayson shook his head, Kevin quickly added, "About that email we discussed."

She said nothing as she stared down at the floor, holding back the flood of emotions that raged within.

Kevin walked through the door and Jayson followed, slamming the door behind him.

Before Kevin could get down the stairs, Jayson had him by the shirt collar. "Now, you listen to me, you shady, manipulative bastard. If you go near her again, I'll not only have your job, but I'll have your head on a platter. Got it?"

Kevin nodded and Jayson shoved him away in disgust. Opening the door, he walked back in to see Lindsey sitting on the sofa, her head in her hands. He sat beside her and put an arm around her shoulder. She flinched.

"It's just me. He's gone." Jayson wanted to comfort her, but he wasn't sure if she would appreciate his attentions.

She looked up and gave him a trembling smile. "Thank you. I don't know what got into him, but I'm glad you were here to stop it." She sniffed. "It's been one hell of a night."

He leaned back on the sofa and tried to appear casual. "Tell me all about it. I have big shoulders. I'm sure I can handle whatever you heap on them."

She gave him a sidelong glance. "I don't know."

"Really, Lindsey." His tone was serious. "I'm here if you need anything. Anytime."

She wiped away a tear. "Thank you. I do appreciate it." Her lips pursed into a straight line. "What if I need you when you're working?"

He tried to keep his face passive. She was setting him up. Even in her disappointment, she was trying to goad him.

He pretended to think about it. "Hmm, are you more important than my work? Is this a trick question?"

She smiled then. "No, I already know the answer. Your work always comes first."

He reached for her hand and gently caressed her palm with his thumb. "You have the softest skin." He hadn't intended to say that out loud, but once he had, he wouldn't apologize for it.

She looked up at him. "Have you been drinking?"

He laughed. "Not a drop. You?"

She shook her head. "None, although a bottle or two of wine seems appropriate about now."

He released a light chuckle. "I have a better idea. How about we go out on the deck and enjoy the stars and fresh air. The ocean is a tremendous ointment for the soul."

"My, what a poet you are. I think you've convinced me."

He stood and gently pulled her up with him, her

hand still in his. Walking around the sofas, they opened the doors and stepped out onto the deck. He was instantly reminded of the night before when he'd found her out there in nothing but her panties and a t-shirt. The empty glass of whiskey at her side. He felt an intense protective urge, and he realized that it was the same feeling he had as he carried her from the deck to her bed the previous evening.

He led her off to the right where a large glider sat in shadow. The sun had already set, but the moon was casting its light in shimmering waves across the water. They sat and watched in silence as the sparkles of light danced and bounced across the tide. She leaned her head on Jayson's shoulder and he put an arm around her. It should have been awkward for both of them, yet she seemed completely relaxed. Jayson thought having her near him, by his side, was the most natural thing he'd ever experienced. That feeling should have terrified him. Instead, he felt that, for the first time in years, all was right in his world.

He felt her shake against him, and he pulled her closer. "Cold?"

She shook her head and sniffed loudly. "No."

She was crying. Dammit all to hell! I'll kill Kevin!

"Do you want to talk about it? If not, you can just cry. It's okay either way. I'm not going anywhere." He gave her a squeeze of support.

She inhaled a deep breath. "I'm sorry. I'm not usually a blubbering baby."

He laughed. "I absolutely believe you. I've never seen

a more self-assured and capable woman in my life."

Her face lifted to his. The moonlight illuminated her features. "Then why am I such a failure? All my life I've fought to be enough. I used to feel guilty because my mom …" she cut off suddenly and swallowed as sob. "My past has been rough; I lost my mom to suicide and I always worried it was because I'd not done enough or played my part correctly. When I grew up, I pushed myself hard to prove to that I could do anything I set my mind to. After college, I worked my ass off at this job, and despite all the obstacles, I was holding my head high. But this interview …" She shook her head. "It was a disaster, Jayson. A complete and utter flop."

He put a hand to her cheek. "It'll work out, one way or another."

"How can you be so sure?" The sadness in her voice was like a knife to his heart.

"Because you are Lindsey Sparks, and Lindsey Sparks is a fighter. Not to mention you have me by your side, ready to fight along with you."

She searched his face for a moment, then closed her eyes, letting a single tear slide from under her thick dark lashes. He used his thumb to wipe it away.

"Lindsey, look at me," he pleaded.

She slowly opened her eyes. Jayson's eyes scanned over every exquisite detail of her face, stopping at her lips. "Lindsey," he whispered, "may I kiss you?"

Her eyes widened for a split second, then she nodded wordlessly.

He gently closed the distance between them and

pressed his lips to hers. He had intended it to be something tender and sweet, but then she parted her lips and he felt the tip of her tongue dart out quickly. His automatic response was to deepen the kiss. She wrapped her arms around his neck, and he pulled her onto his lap. Jayson groaned as he explored her lips, then moved to her cheek and jawline. Her hands slipped under his shirt as they roamed over his flat stomach and the chiseled muscles of his chest. Her touch almost drove him mad. He needed to get closer. Needed to feel her bare skin against his.

She pulled away, and he froze. He dropped his head and felt shame overcome him. "I'm so sorry, Lindsey. I shouldn't have. You've already had to fight off one idiot tonight. You should have to deal with me too."

"Jayson, it's your turn to look at me."

He raised his eyes to hers.

"Please don't compare yourself to Kevin. He didn't ask for permission. He just took without considering my feelings. I didn't want his attention, but with you …" She smiled and gave a bashful shrug. "I know we've had our differences, but I like you."

He smirked. "I knew it."

She swatted his arm. "You did not!"

He laughed. "Okay, maybe I didn't."

Her true smile was back, and he'd do just about anything to assure she kept it. "I love your smile. Especially when it's directed at me."

She raised her hands to the top button on her blouse and slowly worked it free. Her fingers deftly moved to the one below it and did the same. Jayson stared as her hands gradually made their way down the entire row of buttons. She shrugged out of her shirt and tossed it on the chair next to them.

Jayson unfastened the top two buttons of his shirt and pulled it over his head, tossing it next to hers. She reached out to touch him again, and he stopped her hand.

"Are you absolutely sure this is what you want? It's not too late to back out. Ever. I'll always respect your wishes, even if it gives me a raging case of blue balls."

She laughed and nodded. "I'm sure."

He stood and motioned for her to follow him. When she obeyed, he pulled the large pad off the glider and laid it on the deck. He sat on it and tugged her down with him, quickly rolling her so she was pinned beneath him. Her hands began to roam once again and he smiled as he dipped his head to hers for another kiss. His dreams were about to become a reality.

Lindsey woke up the next morning feeling a bit odd. Not a bad odd, just as if something was different. She stretched and rolled over, opened her eyes, and looked directly into the sleeping face of Jayson. His normally spiky hair had flattened a bit and she brushed back a stray couple of strands.

His eyes fluttered open. "Hey, beautiful."

She smiled. "Hi."

"It's not time to get up yet, is it? We can sleep a while longer?" He wrapped an arm around her and pulled her close, nuzzling his face into her neck.

"I have no idea what time it is. The sun is up, though, so we probably should be too."

"No," came his muffled voice from the vicinity of her collar bone. He started kissing her bare skin. In between kisses he said, "We." *Kiss.* "Should." *Kiss.* "Stay" *Kiss.* "In bed." *Kiss.* "All day."

She laughed and squirmed as his hands reached down and lightly touched her sides, finding the ticklish spots he'd discovered the night before. Then he rolled her to her back and sat on top of her, his hands poised over her with wiggling fingers. "I will torture your ticklish spots until you agree to stay in bed with me all day."

She laughed harder as she worked to get free. "Not fair! If I'd had known you would use my only weakness against me, I'd never have let you touch me!"

He leaned down close to her face. "Are you sure that's your only weakness? Might there be some other item that makes you squirm and sigh and moan with helplessness?" He had a devilish glint in his eyes.

She smirked up at him. "Oh, you mean is there something you possess that makes me laugh uncontrollably? Yes, there is that."

"Oh! You are gonna pay for that one!" He grabbed her sides and began to tickle.

She shouted, "Okay, you win! I give!" A deep breath between laughs. "Just stop! I can't stand it!"

Jayson ceased his tickling and smiled down at her as she regained her composure. His face went from smiling to serious in a flash. She stopped smiling. "What is it?"

He stretched out on top of her, intertwining his fingers with hers and pulling her arms above her head. "You. You're it."

She looked puzzled. "Excuse me?"

He gave her a gentle, loving kiss. When he pulled back he looked into her eyes. "I … nothing. Never mind. I'm just being silly."

She kissed the tip of his nose. "That's nothing new."

"You sure know how to wound a guy."

She rolled her eyes. "Oh, this is nothing. Just before I left home, I stapled a co-worker in the nuts for getting handsy."

Jayson rolled off of her and groaned. "Oh, damn. Well, that killed any mood I was working up to."

She turned her head to face him. "It was a long time coming. He deserved that and much more."

"I don't doubt it."

She sighed heavily. "I work with a bunch of horny old goats. I was really looking forward to going back with that interview and shoving it in all their misogynistic faces."

"Oh?" he asked.

"They didn't believe I could do it. I'm sure that's why the boss gave me the assignment. If I fail, he has a loophole to get out of our agreement. I may even lose my job."

"Really? It's that bad?"

"Yeah. But you know what? It's okay. There are other places to work. Hell, this could be a blessing in disguise. It might be what it takes to finally motivate me to move on."

Jayson frowned. "Do you like your current job?"

"Yeah, I suppose I do. I like the work, anyway. It's the idiots I work with and for that make me crazy. I think I believed if I waited them out long enough, most of them would retire, or pass on, and I would be there to step in and take over. I can see now that's likely to never happen."

He continued to frown at her.

"Oh, don't look so gloomy. It's just a job. I'll find something else soon enough. I think I was ready for a new beginning anyway."

"Yeah," he said. "I know how you feel."

Chapter Thirteen

JAYSON LEANED AGAINST the kitchen counter and watched as Lindsey pulled a tin full of blueberry muffins from the oven. He couldn't seem to tear his eyes away from her. Their time together the night before had been amazing. The attraction to each other had been there from the start, but he had never intended to act on it. He suspected Lindsey hadn't, either. Last night took them both by surprise.

He sipped his coffee and closed his eyes. He needed to figure some things out. Lindsey was a stubborn, determined woman that often drove him batty. She was exactly the distraction he feared she'd be. While he'd certainly found some new inspiration, his writing time had taken a severe hit. He was still running behind on his manuscript, especially since his story had taken a new turn.

To complicate matters further, there was Kevin. In the short time Jayson had known him, the man had always appeared driven and innovative. Kevin had never been his favorite person, and now he knew why. His gut had somehow picked up on the manipulative side of Kevin—the side that would do anything to get what he wanted, no matter who he hurt. He'd been angling for Jackson King publicity since the day he signed on. Jayson never dreamed the cad would go as far as setting up an impostor to make it happen. Jayson hated that Lindsey got caught in the middle.

"Jayson, are you okay?" Lindsey's voice broke through his introspection.

"Yeah, I'm good." He stepped to her side to grab a plate and a muffin.

"Are you sure? You were frowning into your coffee like it was the most offensive thing you've ever seen." He flashed her a reassuring smile. "I promise. I'm good." He leaned toward her and gave her a quick peck on the forehead. Grabbing his plate, he made his way through the living room and out onto the deck. He watched the waves roll in as he took a bite of his breakfast.

"Lord have mercy! Where did you learn to make muffins that taste like euphoria?" His mouth was full as he complimented her baking skills.

She sat next to him with her own plate and smiled. "Euphoria is the secret ingredient. Very hard to find." She licked a crumb off of her finger. "You can't just grow it in a garden, you know."

He answered with a smirk, all his previous concerns temporarily forgotten. "I'd imagine it isn't. Tell me, do you have to take a sacred quest to obtain such a valuable ingredient?"

"No, you just have to know where to look." She winked at him.

"Then you have a map of some sort?" He knew this conversation was ridiculous, but he was enjoying the levity of it.

"I might have a map. I might even be persuaded to show it to you." The corner of her mouth curved up in a secretive smile.

"Really?" He shoved the last bite of muffin into his mouth. After swallowing, he added, "And just what would I need to do to convince you?"

She turned to face him fully, then leaned forward to whisper near his ear. "A replay of last night wouldn't hurt."

His eyes lit up. "Really? I'm sure something can be arranged." He would have loved to drag her to her bedroom in that moment and make good on her request, but responsibilities were calling. "But we'll have to save it for tonight. I still have to get some work done."

He winced when he saw her smile fade. Work. The entire reason she was there, and reason she'd likely be going home soon. He felt a lump in his throat at the thought. He'd only known her a little over a week, but the idea of being alone in the house, or more specifically, being without her, left an ache in his chest. He also felt guilty. He could easily solve her problem, but then that would create a larger problem for him. He had no intention of the public ever finding out about his past. It would only aggravate an already intensely complicated relationship with Pete. It really wasn't an option he could explore.

Jayson cleared his throat. "Do you have any plans for today?"

She picked at her muffin quietly. For a moment, he thought she wouldn't answer. "I guess I'm going to do some job hunting on the Internet, maybe read a book on the beach. I don't really know yet."

He nodded. "The reading sounds nice. It's been a while since I just relaxed with a good book." His reading time had been cut short with recent deadlines, and he was looking forward to some downtime once he turned in this manuscript.

She attempted a smile. "Well, I just finished the latest Jackson King. If you're interested, it's on my dresser."

He was unsure how to answer that, so he simply said, "Thanks."

Lindsey stood. "I think I'll give Whitney a call. I haven't talked to her for days. Nothing like a little best friend time to get me motivated again."

He nodded and stood as well. She turned to walk away but he grabbed her hand and pulled her close. "I'll be closeted away for a while. I thought maybe I should get a kiss to tide me over."

She smirked. "You probably should. But I wouldn't want to plant distracting thoughts in your head, so we should probably wait until later." She pulled away and stepped through the door.

He called after her, "You do realize you just made the distraction worse, right?"

She continued to walk away, but shrugged as if to say, "Oh, well."

"Frustrating little minx," he grumbled.

Lindsey hung up the phone and sighed. Her talk with Whitney was long overdue. She felt better after confiding in her best friend about all the chaos she'd been through, including the mix up with the house. Whitney had mentioned that Aidan was probably going to wig out on Simon Jay the next time they spoke, but Lindsey assured her it all worked out fine and for them not to worry about it.

She roamed through the house looking for something to read on the beach. There had to be something in the house she hadn't read yet. As she scanned a small bookshelf filled with a variety of classic literature, she heard her phone ring. The caller ID announced that it was Kevin. For a split second, she considered letting it go to voicemail, but changed her mind and answered.

"This is Lindsey."

"Hi, Lindsey, it's Kevin. But I guess you probably knew that already."

She exhaled a heavy sigh. "What do you want?"

"I first want to apologize. I never should have been so pushy last night. I'm not really sure what came over me."

"Uh huh."

"Really, I'm deeply sorry. I know that doesn't excuse my behavior, but I wanted to make sure you knew that I regret my actions."

"Let's just move past that, Kevin. Anything else?"

"Yes." He was silent momentarily. "We have something important to discuss."

"Honestly, Kevin, I don't think we do." She was rapidly getting tired of their conversation.

"We do, Lindsey. I can't talk to you about it over the phone, but it's important." He paused. "Please, just hear me out. We can meet in public, and I promise to leave you alone when all is said and done, if you want me to."

She chewed on her bottom lip as she thought it over. The idea of spending time with Kevin no longer appealed to her. No doubt Jayson would have a fit if he thought she was meeting him anywhere. Not because they owed each other anything, but because Jayson seemed to be instinctively protective of her. She liked that about him, yet it also irked her. She wasn't helpless, despite her issue with Kevin the previous night.

"Lindsey? Please?"

"Fine. Where and when?" Her heart said it was a bad idea, but her mind wasn't as easily convinced. Maybe it would be good to find out what he wanted, then get some closure on the whole Kevin and Jackson King mess.

"I have some things to take care of today, but how

about we meet at The Shaka Bar around five thirty. I'll text you the directions."

"Sure. See you then."

"Thanks, Lindsey. I appreciate your time. Have a nice day."

"You too." She hung up the phone and wondered if she was making a huge mistake. There was no way she was telling Jayson, not that it was really any of his business anyway.

Lindsey went back to searching for something to read when she stumbled onto a copy of *To Kill a Mockingbird* by Harper Lee. *Perfect! Not new to me, but I haven't read this in years!* She packed the book in her tote bag, along with some sunscreen, a towel, and her cell phone. She stared at the phone for a few seconds and decided to leave it on the kitchen counter. She was officially on vacation time, at least until she figured out her next move. She didn't want someone to interrupt her afternoon of reading.

Jayson typed away on his laptop, the words coming faster than he could put them on the screen. Lindsey had somehow become his greatest muse, as well as his greatest distraction. Their time together the previous night had been a catalyst for his motivation. He felt invigorated. The heroine in his story was shaping up to be a lot like Lindsey, at least in character. Determined, sarcastic, funny—she was also beautiful, but with different features. He had to stay true to his original character, after all.

He spent the entire afternoon engrossed in his work, so much so that he'd skipped lunch completely. His stomach had no problem reminding him that nourishment was important, so he saved his work and went downstairs for a snack. He was also looking forward to seeing Lindsey. He hoped they could have a quiet dinner together that evening and let things progress naturally. He knew they'd end up in bed eventually—there was too much passion between them to deny it. *Take that,* Kevin*! She thinks I'm better than fine!* He smirked at his inner taunting. He was thinking like a jealous man, or at the least, a guy that disliked competition. If he were truthful, it was probably a bit of both.

He entered the kitchen and rummaged through the cabinets until he found some peanut butter crackers. He'd just torn open the package when he heard high-pitched chime sounds behind him. Jayson turned to see Lindsey's cell phone vibrating.

He called out. "Lindsey? Your phone is going off!" He glanced down at the screen. "I think it's a text message!"

No answer. He frowned. *Where is she?* He knocked on her door, but again, no answer, so he quietly and slowly pushed the door open. The room was empty and her bed was made. He checked the bathroom as well, but it was also vacant.

Stepping back into the living area, he glanced out of the window and saw her lying on a beach chair. It appeared she was reading. He smiled. *Good, she needed to relax.*

Her text tone went off again, and Jayson wondered if it was something important. He decided it wouldn't hurt to peek at the screen to be sure. He approached the counter and picked up her phone. The screen lit up once again and bells chimed. On the screen, he saw a message from someone named Shawn.

Lindsey, please talk to me. You know this time apart isn't good for either of us. Come back home and let me make it up to you. We were meant to be together.

He frowned and went back into the kitchen to get a drink, her cell phone still in his hand. He stood at the fridge for a few minutes and tried to keep his mind from going rogue. It wasn't fair to judge a situation by a text. *Is this the guy sexting her a few days ago?* He grabbed a soda and walked back into the living room.

"Who the hell is Shawn?" he muttered out loud.

Lindsey spoke up just as she walked through the French doors. "Shawn is an ex of mine. Why do you have my phone, and why are you reading my messages?" The annoyance in her voice was unmistakable.

"I was making sure it wasn't important."

She raised an eyebrow, her face completely void of any humor. "And how would you know if it were important or not?" She stepped forward and snatched the phone from his hands. "Do you make it habit of going through other people's phones?"

"No, I don't." His jaw clenched in irritation. *How dare she accuse me of doing something inappropriate?* He raised his voice a bit. "I was trying to help!"

"Help?" The pitch of her voice increased as well. "Why do I need your help? Did I ask for it?" She jabbed a finger in his chest. "Do I seem helpless to you?" She jabbed him again. "Why do all the men I know seem to assume I can't think for *myself*?"

"Lindsey, it's just a text message. I couldn't help but see it since your damn phone displays the thing every time one arrives." He was trying to be rational and hoped she'd see reason too.

"Maybe *you* should keep your eyeballs off my phone then!" She shoved it in the tote bag hanging off her shoulder.

"Maybe *you* should put your damn phone up! Especially if you're gonna freak out over something so stupid."

"What?" Her voice trembled. "My expectation to privacy isn't stupid."

"Well, you kinda blew that expectation when you agreed to live with a man you don't even know!" His temper was mounting, but he couldn't seem to stop himself.

"Oh, you are such a jerk!" she screamed.

"You didn't seem to think so last night," he stated.

"Don't you dare throw that in my face. Last night was obviously a big mistake."

"Last night?" He laughed incredulously. "This whole damn week was a big mistake. I should have stuck to my guns and insisted you leave. I mean seriously, who agrees to live with a guy she doesn't know? I could have been a psycho!"

She threw her arms up in the air. "Who says you aren't?"

She was still close enough to touch, and he wanted to throttle her. Without thinking, he grabbed her upper arms and pulled her close. His hand threaded through her hair, and he pulled her face to his for a punishing kiss. He poured all of his frustration and passion into the action, and for a moment, she tensed, but promptly relaxed and returned in kind. He picked her up and set her on the counter, wedging himself between her legs. His hands roamed the soft skin her bikini left bare. He reached up to untie the back and she stiffened.

"No. We aren't doing this." She pushed him away and slid down until her feet touched the floor.

He ran his fingers through his hair. "Listen… I didn't…"

She raised her hand to cut him off. "It doesn't matter. We can talk later. I have to get ready to go." She turned and moved toward her bedroom.

He frowned. "Where are you going?"

She reached her door, then turned to face him. "It's really none of your business."

He knew she was right, yet he couldn't let it go. "Shouldn't you leave an address or destination in case something happens?"

"I tell you I have plans, and you assume I'm going to run straight into trouble?" She shook her head. "You don't know me well enough to doubt me, Jayson."

His frown deepened. "I don't know you well enough to trust you, either."

She nodded in agreement. "True. So maybe you should worry about you, and I'll worry about me." She entered her room and slammed the door.

Well, that went splendidly. That argument went from minor to major in a flash. He no longer had an appetite, so he grabbed his bottle of soda and left the crackers on the counter. On the way up the stairs, he wondered if it was too late to make his heroine the villain instead. His inspiration for her was sure turning out to be a pain in his ass.

Chapter Fourteen

LINDSEY FOLLOWED THE directions Kevin gave her and arrived at the bar at twenty after five. The open air bar was a fun little place right on the beach. Tables and umbrellas dotted the area around the bar itself, so Lindsey chose an empty one and sat down. On any other day, it would have been just her kind of place to hang out—drinks, music, and everyone enjoying themselves as they watched the sunset. But instead, she was there to hear Kevin out, make peace with her failure, and move on.

She thought about her fight with Jayson as she waited. Sometimes, he really pissed her off. He seemed almost like Jekyll and Hyde. One moment he was considerate and sweet, the next moment he was telling her what to do, who to see, and snooping on her phone. His arrogant presumption over her best interests really struck a nerve. All her life she'd fought to get to the place where she was making her own decisions. Even if they were sometimes mistakes, at least they were her mistakes to own and learn from. Sadly, when it came to men, she felt like she was once again falling back into her old pattern.

To be fair, Jayson hadn't been totally wrong about Kevin. It was nice of Kevin to work on her interview, but outside of that, he'd shown a side of himself she didn't care for. Sure, he apologized, but he had had no right to assume she wanted his advances. *Aren't you being a little hypocritical?* her inner voice asked. *Didn't Jayson take the same liberties this afternoon during your fight?* It wasn't quite the same. They had slept together the night before after all. He certainly had more right to expect her attention than Kevin had. And, if she would admit it, that kiss was kinda hot. But she knew Jayson's type. He'd either get tired of her and move on to the next girl, or he'd decide to stay and try to run her life. And that was assuming they even attempted to maintain a relationship once she went back to Indiana.

She shook her head and looked into the margarita she'd ordered before she sat down. A shadow crossed her table, and she looked up.

Kevin stood next to the table, his hands in the pockets of his trousers. He was fidgeting, and she could hear the keys and change rattle as he twitched his fingers.

"Please, sit down." She gestured to the seat across from her.

Kevin obliged, then placed both hands in front of him on the table. He lightly drummed his fingers as he looked at her.

"Well? What's so damn important that you couldn't tell me on the phone?" His nervousness was already rubbing of on her and she was getting impatient.

"It's about Jackson King." His mouth formed a grim line.

"What about him? I told you not to bother that poor man. Is he okay?"

"Lindsey, he's fine, but the man you met is not Jackson King."

Her eyes went wide. "But … what are you talking about? Why would you set up an interview with the wrong guy?"

"Because the real Jackson King does not want to be interviewed, at least, not in person. He prefers no personal details of any kind be shared or leaked to the press. I could lose my job for even telling you what I'm about to tell you."

"Then why are you telling me?" She asked.

"Because you're a nice person, and you deserve to know. All I ask is that what I'm about to tell you goes no further than you and I."

"You mean, don't publish anything you tell me?"

He nodded. "That, and don't tell a soul about this secret."

"Okay." She wasn't sure what she was agreeing to, but she'd do her best to keep her promise.

"The man you met was an intern. I thought he fit the look and could pull it off, but he got nervous when your questions became more personal. He lost his nerve and ran. I apologize for trying to deceive you. It's just … that pompous turd wouldn't help you, and it made me mad."

"You mean Mr. King?" She wasn't sure where he was going with his confession, but she was trying to keep up.

"Yes, Jackson King, except that's not his real name—it's a pen name. His real name—" he paused. "His real name is Jayson Conway."

Her mouth fell open, and the shock of his words hit her hard. "You mean my Jayson?"

He nodded once again. "I'm sorry. I should have told you when I realized he was your house-mate."

She felt numb. *Jayson? All this time?* He knew how much the interview had meant to her. *Why didn't he just tell me? This can't be true!*

"You're lying," she accused.

"No, I swear to God. I'm telling the truth."

She studied his face, hoping to find some tell that gave away his deceit. Not that she was any kind of expert on micro-expressions or any such science, but surely if he were lying there would be some kind of clue. *If only pants really did catch on fire when someone was a liar.*

He looked sincere, and she hated him for it. That meant that Jayson was indeed Jackson King, and she was officially a fool.

Lindsey walked through the door of the beach house two hours later. Her mind was whirling. There had to be some mix up. She'd driven around the island for an hour, going nowhere in particular, just to be alone with her thoughts. She still couldn't believe Jayson would deceive her in such a way. But then, as she pointed out earlier, they didn't really know each other all that well. It was certainly not an impossible notion.

She stopped and listened for movement upstairs, but heard nothing. Come to think of it, she hadn't seen lights on in the upper floor when she pulled up. It appeared he wasn't home.

She slipped off her shoes and walked through the house until she reached her bedroom. The door was open, a letter placed on her pillow. She sat her purse on the bed and walked toward the headboard. Her first instinct was to tear the letter up, but a small part of her still wished it all to be a cruel joke, so she gave in to hope and opened the letter.

Lindsey,

 I need to apologize. I swear I wasn't trying to invade your privacy or spy on you. I was afraid you were missing an important message, but you were right. I should have left it alone.

 I don't know why sometimes we get along, but other times are at each other's throats. I do know we are both a little stubborn, and that always causes some friction. I hope you'll forgive me and we can be friends again.

Jayson

Friends? Is that what we are? She frowned down at the letter in her hands. That was probably the most accurate description of their relationship, with the exception of the night before. Friends don't usually have sex, at least not the kind of friends she preferred to associate with. Her mind flashed back to Kevin and his recent admission. If he was telling the truth, then even friends was being too generous.

She heard the front door open, so she tossed the letter on the bed and went to her door. Poking her head around the corner, she saw Jayson enter the house and close the door behind him. *Should I confront him?* Her heart raced at the thought. Confronting him meant knowing the truth, and she wasn't sure she was ready to hear it from him. Then her mind flashed back to the moment she'd picked up his reading material and he'd become defensive. She'd asked if he wrote it, but he avoided the question. There was also the odd confrontational vibe between Kevin and Jayson at dinner that night. She felt a little sick to her stomach.

"Lindsey? Are you home?" Jayson's voice echoed through the living room.

She stepped out of her room, and in a soft voice, said, "I'm here."

He smiled at her, but it didn't take long to fade. "What's wrong? What happened?"

She shrugged. "Nothing much, really. I had a drink, talked to some people, drove around the island, and then came home."

"Okay. So why do you look like someone shot your dog? Are you still upset about our fight? Did you get my letter?"

The concern on his face appeared to be real, but she no longer trusted her character judgment. She walked toward him until she was close enough she could touch him.

"No, I'm not upset over that." She looked up into his eyes. "Tell me, Jayson, what do you do for a living?"

He rubbed his forehead, effectively keeping her from maintaining eye contact. "Nothing special, why?"

"Why? Well, I did sleep with you last night. I think I at least deserve to know your occupation. Or is that one of those things that a girl learns after the second tumble?"

He smirked. "Well, I'm glad to see some of your spunk return. That quiet mousy routine just isn't you."

"Ya know, you're right. It isn't me at all. I'm more forceful, loud, and sometimes even violent. Are you sure that's the side of me you want to see right now?"

His eyes squinted in suspicion. "Why do I have the feeling I'm being set up here."

She crossed her arms and spoke succinctly. "What. Do. You. Do?"

He backed away from her and entered the kitchen. She was hot on his heels. "Don't walk away from me. I'm asking you a question. You can't ignore it!"

He opened a beer and took a drink. "Can't I? Looks like I just did."

She leaned against the counter. "I take it you're afraid I'll beg you to give me an exclusive on your next spy thriller?"

Jayson lowered his beer.

"Don't worry, Mr. King; I'm done chasing you down." She turned away from him and left the kitchen.

She entered her bedroom, slipped on her shoes, and hauled her suitcase up onto the bed. She unzipped the main compartment and started tossing clothes in.

Jayson appeared in the doorway. "Lindsey, I can explain."

"No, I don't think you can. Otherwise, you would have told me the truth from the beginning." She felt the sting of tears form in her eyes, and she turned away from him and swiped at them.

"I couldn't." He watched her continue to throw clothes into her suitcase.

"The same way you couldn't tell me you weren't Jay Walsh?" She entered the bathroom to pack up her toiletries.

He sighed. "That was a misunderstanding," he called after her. "The Jackson King thing is very complicated."

"It's not so complicated that you didn't mind letting me blather on and on about what this meant to my career. Or how disappointed I was that I'd failed." She tossed the last of her belongings into the suitcase and zipped it shut.

He stepped forward and put a hand over hers. "Lindsey, please. Just give me a chance to explain."

She shook her head. "I've been here over a week. You've had plenty of time to tell me the truth." She sighed. "If you had just told me, Jayson, I would have tried to understand. I would have heard you out. But it's too late for that now. There's been too many secrets."

She pulled her case off of the bed and set it on its rollers, then grabbed her purse and tried to walk past him.

He stepped backward in a flash and blocked the door. "Where are you going?"

"To a hotel."

"Don't go."

"I have to, Jayson. I can't stay here another minute."

She pushed to get him out of the way, and he stepped back. She pulled her case to the front door and he followed behind. "I promise to stay upstairs and completely out of your way. Just don't go."

She kept walking, attempting to ignore him.

"Lindsey, I mean it. I'll give you space. I'll give you some time. Just stay here."

She opened her trunk and tossed her suitcase inside. Closing the trunk, she turned to face him. "Why should I stay? There is nothing for me here."

He searched her face. "Nothing at all?"

Her sad features hardened. "No, nothing at all." She jerked open the driver's side door. "Not anymore. I'm flying home tomorrow. Have a nice life, Jayson, or Jackson—whoever you are. Don't worry, your secret is safe with me."

She lowered herself into the seat, shut the door, and

pulled away. Lindsey glanced back one last time to see Jayson standing in the driveway, watching her leave.

Jayson awoke to the sound of drums. *Drums? Why do I hear drums?* He groaned and rolled over. The sound persisted. He rubbed his eyes and sat up. *Not drums. Someone is pounding on the door.* He looked at his alarm clock. *Hell, I overslept. It's almost nine.*

He slipped into his sweat pants and carefully traversed the stairs until he'd reached the bottom. The pounding persisted.

"Hold your damn horses! I'm coming!" His gruff voice matched is attitude. He was not in the mood for anyone.

He unlocked then swung open the door to see Kevin standing on the other side.

"What the hell do you want?" It was a little early in the day for murder, but he felt sure he could make an exception in Kevin's case.

"I need to see Lindsey." Kevin looked ready to bolt at any moment.

"She's not here, you ass monkey."

Kevin frowned. "Where did she go?"

"Back home, not that it's any of your business."

Kevin looked down at the sunglasses in his hand, and Jayson realized they looked familiar. "Those are Lindsey's."

"Yes, she left them on the table last night. I didn't realize it until she'd already driven away."

Kevin turned to leave, but Jayson grabbed the back of his collar and pulled him inside. "It was you, wasn't it? You told her I was Jackson King."

"What?" he choked. "I can't do that. It's a breach of contract." His smoothed his shirt calmly as Jayson relinquished his hold on the fabric.

"But you did anyway. You told her because you're jealous and pissed at me."

"Jealous? What do I have to be jealous about?"

"My relationship with Lindsey."

Kevin snorted.

"Do you deny it?"

"I'm done with this conversation." Kevin turned to leave.

"Good, I'm glad to hear it, Simpson. You're also done in the world of publishing. Breach of contract is considered an actionable offense."

Kevin froze for a moment, then he straightened his spine and said, "At least I didn't cost Lindsey *her* job. That one is on you." He walked out of the door without another word.

Chapter Fifteen

LINDSEY SAT AT her desk and worked on the recipe section of the magazine. She had to have four new recipes for the next month's issue, and she was having a difficult time finding something original.

"Hey, Lindsey? A few of us are going out to Rowdy Doc's after work. Wanna join us?"

She smiled up at the lovely young intern. "No, thanks, Maggie. I have a lot to finish up tonight."

"Aw, c'mon. You've been holed up in this office every weeknight for the past month. Ever since you came back from that trip, you haven't quite been yourself. Is everything okay?"

"Everything is fine. I promise." She almost choked on the word fine. It was fine, but it wasn't great. She missed great.

"Okay then. If you change your mind, we'd love to have you join us." Maggie patted Lindsey on the arm as she walked away.

Lindsey rubbed her temples. Everyone noticed the change in her. Everyone except Lindsey herself. She had no idea what they were talking about. Sure, she'd been spending more time at work than usual, but she was twenty-five and not getting any younger. It felt like the right time to totally focus on her career. The parties and bars were no longer as appealing as they once were.

She expected Mr. Clayton to find a reason to fire her once she'd returned with nothing but an expense bill. He surprised her by smiling and saying, "No harm, no foul, sweetheart. You tried." He'd put her back into her old position of writing fluff pieces. It wasn't what she wanted, but it would have to do until she found another job.

The work day was almost over, but Lindsey didn't want to go home. Her time in Florida only accentuated how lonely her apartment really was. She tried not to miss Jayson, but every so often she'd see a sandwich and think of the day she'd almost killed him with a plant. Or pick up asparagus and remember his outrageous bias against vegetables. The nights were even worse; she often dreamed of him. Sometimes the dreams were wonderful, other times they were nightmares. He was ruining her happiness, and he wasn't even there.

She shut down her computer and grabbed her things. On her way to the elevator, she pulled out her cell and called Whitney.

"Hey, Whit! I need a drink, are you free tonight?"

"Well," started Whitney, "Aidan and I were going to talk wedding stuff tonight, but I'm sure that can wait until tomorrow. *Oh*. Or you can help! Come on over, and I'll put you to work!"

Lindsey laughed. "Sweetie, a drunk me helping plan your wedding is either an amazing idea, or the worst thing you've ever suggested."

"Well, get your butt over here, and let's find out which it is!"

Lindsey sat in the spacious living room of the home Whitney and Aidan shared. It was a newer-style ranch house with some of the most luxurious leather furniture Lindsey had ever sank into.

"I swear, this sofa is making love to me. I want to stay here forever and have its children."

Whitney rolled her eyes and looked at Aidan. "Well, it's obvious Lindsey has had enough wine."

Aidan tried to suppress a grin.

"I know that look. What are you thinking?" Whitney asked him as she sorted through bridal magazines.

"I was trying to envision sofa children. Would they look like, Lindsey? Or would they look more like the sofa?"

Whitney bit her lip. "Oh, lord. Lindsey, can you imagine pushing a sofa out of your—"

"Okay! That's enough! Even the drunk lady has her limits. I don't want to think of pushing anything out of my anything."

Aidan put his hands in his face. "I'm sorry I started this line of thought. I can't un-hear any of that."

Lindsey rocked herself forward and stood up. She was surprisingly steady, despite having a little too much wine. "I've gotta visit the little girl's room. I'll be back."

She had to walk past the kitchen to reach the hallway and guest bathroom. As she passed the breakfast bar, she noticed something with her name on it and backed up. Picking up the stack of letters, she saw they were all addressed to her.

"Whitney? Get your skinny ass in here and explain this," she shouted a little too loudly. She was suddenly glad Caleb was at a sleepover. It wouldn't do for him to see Auntie Lindsey shouting and stumbling like a lush.

Whitney entered the kitchen and stopped when she saw the envelopes in Lindsey's hands. "Oh. Those."

"Why do you have letters with my name but your address?"

"Well, we didn't know if you were ready for those, or if you'd even want them. He didn't have your address, so he talked to Simon Jay, who in turn gave him our address so they'd get to you."

Lindsey looked confused.

"They're from Jayson," Whitney clarified.

"Oh." That was all she could say. From the looks of it, Jayson had written several times a week.

"I'm sorry, Lindsey. We should have told you earlier, but you've just been … I don't know, just not yourself since you returned. And I know you said things ended badly with him and you never wanted to see him again. If he's the source of your sadness, I wanted to protect you from that as long as possible. But I kept them, just in case you changed your mind someday."

Lindsey pulled Whitney close for a hug. "I know you are always looking out for me, even when I'm behaving like an idiot. Do you know how much I love you for that?"

Whitney smiled. "Hopefully as much as I love you."

"You got it, sister!" Lindsey pulled away then blew Whitney a kiss and strolled back into the living room with the letters in hand. She shoved them into her purse, determined to deal with them the next day … maybe.

Lindsey woke up with a headache and chastised herself for the overindulgence at Whitney's the night before. She muttered to herself, "Get up, ya bum. You just have to get through today, then you can spend the weekend with two of your closest friends—chocolate and old movies." Wine was not getting an invite. She needed to put the brakes on her drinking for a bit. She rolled over and glanced at her clock. "Crap! I'm late!"

She showered, dressed, and ate breakfast in record time, then popped two ibuprofen as she headed out the door. She'd made it to work only a couple of minutes late, but there was no telling if Mr. Clayton would look past it or lay into her. She had to admit, he'd been especially genial since her confrontation with him in his office. Maybe he still worried she'd follow through on that lawsuit. Whatever the cause, she'd take it and appreciate it.

"Miss Sparks!" Mr. Clayton's voice bellowed across the large space. "In my office! Now!"

"Well," she thought, *"that was short lived."* Lindsey put her purse under her desk and headed straight for Mr. Clayton's office. Before she'd even made it to the receptionists' desk, Kathryn held up a hand written sign that said RUN. Lindsey smiled at her but walked through his office doors anyway.

He turned to look at her. "What did you do?" He looked ready to spit nails.

She crossed her arms, refusing to let his blustering intimidate her. "I have no idea what you're talking about. I've done lots of things. I need more detail."

"Don't get cheeky with me, missy! I just got a call saying the company lawyers would be here any minute and are requesting a meeting with the both of us."

"Really? That's interesting. Sadly, it's not my doing, so I'm as clueless as you."

He pointed a short stubby finger at her. "If you think I'm going to sit by and watch you besmirch the name of this good company …"

She opened her mouth, but an unfamiliar voice spoke instead. "Miss Sparks, Mr. Clayton, thank you for seeing us on such short notice. I'm Carson, and this Baxter." Turning, she saw two men in expensive suits standing in the doorway. The dark-haired man named Carson motioned for them to take a seat.

Once everyone was settled, the taller of the two men, Baxter, pulled a manila envelope out of his briefcase and handed it to Mr. Clayton.

"What's this?" asked Mr. Clayton.

Baxter gave him a tight smile. "It's your severance package."

"My *what*?" boomed Mr. Clayton. "Why am I getting a severance package?"

It was Carson's turn to smile. "Because you are no longer employed at ICM."

Mr. Clayton stood, his hand shaking in outrage. "How is this possible? For what credible reason am I being terminated?"

"Don't look at is as termination, Mr. Clayton. Consider it early retirement, unless, of course, you prefer to work elsewhere, outside of our non-compete area, obviously." Carson appeared to be enjoying Mr. Clayton's distress.

"I will not stand for this!" bellowed Mr. Clayton.

Baxter stood then. "You will. I strongly suggest you go home, pour yourself a drink, and carefully read over the details of your severance before you say something you can't take back."

Mr. Clayton glanced at the envelope in his hand.

Carson spoke up. "You and your network of hand-picked buddies have been a liability to this company for too long. It's the express wishes of Mr. Pennington, the owner of ICM, that you vacate the premises as soon as possible."

"It's the most generous offer you're going to get," Baxter warned.

Mr. Clayton nodded and grabbed his keys from his desk. "I'll just take the day to look things over."

"Smart man," said Carson.

Mr. Clayton shuffled from the office looking like a kid that'd just lost his balloon. Kathryn had to stifle a laugh when she saw his expression of shock. She'd heard the entire conversation and seemed to be pleased by the outcome.

Lindsey was more than baffled by what just occurred. She turned to the two men looking at her expectantly. "Why did you need me here?"

Carson handed an envelope to her as well. "Mr. Pennington has been looking over the accounts and saw where many of your contributions had increased revenue. He's very impressed."

She shook her head. "Wait, my contributions? I'll be honest, gentlemen, all my ideas did work, but the credit was given to others."

"That has been remedied," Baxter stated.

"But how?"

Baxter gave her a reassuring smile. "Don't worry yourself about the details, Miss Sparks. What you have in your hands is a proposal. Mr. Pennington would like you to consider taking over Mr. Clayton's position. He feels you are the most qualified and would run the office in an organized and professional manner."

"Seriously? He wants me?" She could hardly believe her ears. That was one hell of a promotion.

"Seriously," said Carson.

"I don't know what to say?"

Baxter released a small chuckle. "Say you'll look at the proposal and consider the job."

"For now, though," Carson interjected, "it's been requested that you also take the day to consider your options while we do some house cleaning here."

"House cleaning?"

"Yes, ma'am," said Baxter. "Some of the other liabilities need to be dealt with. We assure you none of the truly valuable employees will be let go."

She smiled at them both and rose from her chair. "Thank you so much, gentleman. I'll get back with you tomorrow, if that's acceptable."

They stood as well and both reached out to shake her hand. "That'd be perfect."

Lindsey's commute home seemed to fly by in a haze. She couldn't believe her luck. Mr. Clayton gone. His cronies gone. A new, higher paying position doing what she loved. *It's almost perfect.*

Once at her apartment building, she inserted the key into her lock and screamed as she felt someone come up behind her. She swung and her fist collided with someone's face.

"Ouch! Who taught you that right hook?" Jayson leaned against the wall and held a hand over his eye.

"Jayson?" She couldn't believe he was there.

"Yeah, it's me."

She stood there staring at him as if he were an apparition.

"Would it be okay if I came in?" he asked. "I need to put some ice on this eye before it swells up."

"Oh! Yes! So sorry!" She hurried to finish unlocking the door and then ushered him inside.

Lindsey led him to a love seat, then ran to her freezer to bring back an icepack.

He placed it on his left eye and looked at her with his right eye. "You never answered my letters. I didn't know how else to get a hold of you, so I did the douchey thing and called your best friend. It took a lot of convincing to get her to give me your address."

She smirked at him. "That's because she's my best friend. Did she also tell you she didn't give me the letters until last night?"

"No, she left that part out. Now I don't feel bad for pestering her."

"Shut up and keep the ice on your eye. And why the hell were you sneaking up on me like that?" she countered.

"Do you want me to answer or shut up? I can't do both."

"Can't you? I'm pretty sure it's easy for someone that's two-faced."

He lowered the ice pack. "I'm not two-faced, Lindsey. I'm just in a difficult situation. I explained it all in the letters I sent you."

"Well, I didn't see them, so why don't you explain it

now." She sat in the chair across from him and waited.

He nodded and took a deep breath. "I love writing, but I don't want to be in the spotlight." He studied her a moment. "Have you ever done something you regret? I mean deeply, deeply regret?"

She nodded. "I think most people have. It's human nature to screw up."

"True," he said, "but some screw-ups are way bigger than others. Mine was a colossal lack of judgment. It's the kind of thing that could potentially destroy a person should the media get a hold of it. That's why I don't grant in-person interviews or put a picture of myself on the jacket."

Lindsey frowned. "C'mon. It can't be that bad, can it? I mean, you didn't kill someone, right?"

His sorrowful expression deepened, but he didn't answer.

"Jayson? What happened?" Apprehension filled her voice.

"Do you still have the letters?"

She nodded. "They're on the table."

"Read the first one. Take some time to think about what you've learned. When you're ready to talk more, let me know." He stood and handed her the ice pack. "Thanks for giving me your time."

She watched him leave without saying a word. *Oh, lord. What could be so awful that he can't even say it to my face?* She glanced at the stack of letters on the table, unsure if she wanted to open that particular can of worms. She knew that once she learned whatever it was, she couldn't put it back.

She slowly rose and made her way to the small pile on the table. She picked them up and went back to love seat Jayson had just vacated. Her hands trembled slightly as she opened the first letter.

Lindsey,

I've tried to write this letter several times, but I always hate what I end up with and I start over. This is the final try, because no matter what I say, it's going to be difficult. It's hard to make this admission to someone face to face, and putting it on paper feels like I'm signing away my security. Despite my fears, I'm choosing to tell you the truth.

When I was 16 I ran with the wrong crowd. I was getting into trouble, skipping school, and generally just being an idiot. My mom passed away when I was ten and my dad didn't handle it well. I might as well have been orphaned at that point—I was allowed to do whatever I wanted. He didn't care as long as he had booze. One night my friends and I raided his liquor cabinet and got wasted. There we were, the four of us sitting in the living room drinking until we were three sheets to the wind. The next thing I knew I woke up in the driver's seat of a car I didn't recognize, which was wrapped around a tree. My best friend Mark was in the passenger seat - out cold and bleeding profusely. My other buddy Greg was moaning in the back seat. Dylan was outside of the car sitting on the ground and screaming for help.

The ambulances arrived and eventually we were all transported to the hospital. Mark died before they could get him to the emergency room.

Lindsey, I killed my best friend. It wasn't intentional, but I did it just the same. My dad had money and influence, so he managed to work it out where I only spent time in a juvenile detention center. By age 18 I was out and trying to start a new life. I'll never forgive myself for what happened, but I know Mark would have wanted me to make something of myself. It's in his memory that I push forward. I send his father money every month. He's never forgiven me, and I don't really expect him to, but at least I can honor Mark by taking care of his dad.

Mark's dad doesn't know about my profession. Neither does anyone else that knows the truth about that night. It was a stupid, stupid decision to get behind that wheel that night. I don't know why we decided to leave the house. It's all a blur, but I know Mark is gone and nothing I can do will ever change that.

I hope this explains why I've insisted on

keeping my job and my real identity separate. I have no doubt that a resourceful reporter could dig up all the details once they got a hold of my real name.

I realized after you left that I should have trusted you and explained my situation. I know you aren't into sensationalism and you report with integrity and responsibility.

I'm sorry. I hope you'll find it in your heart to forgive me.

Jayson

Lindsey dropped the letter and took a moment to let his words sink in. His demand for privacy certainly made more sense. But could she look past his deceit? She wasn't sure.

Chapter Sixteen

JAYSON WALKED THROUGH the front door of the beach house with the latest changes from his editor in hand. He really needed to get the edits done as soon as possible, but he found it hard to concentrate. The place that once had felt like paradise was cold and empty. He missed her laugh. He missed her wit. He even missed her insults. He missed *her*. Lindsey hadn't contacted him since the day he visited her apartment. It'd been over two weeks, and he had to assume she was totally done with him.

There were several times when he wondered if he'd made the right decision by telling Lindsey the truth, but he always came back to the fact that she was trustworthy. And if it turned out that she wasn't—well, he was probably getting what he deserved anyway. Either way, he refused to regret telling the woman he loved about something so personal. He'd never been in love before, but he was pretty sure this was what it felt like. It was wonderful and horrible all at once.

He sat his work on the coffee table and took a deep breath. That was when he saw the letter with his name on it. He picked it up and tore into the envelope, letting it fall to the floor as he unfolded the stationary.

Jayson,

Thank you for telling me the truth, because I know you really didn't have to. I now fully understand why you are so secretive about your personal information and I respect that.

After your first letter, I decided to read the others. Thank you for pulling some strings and making sure that Mr. Pennington got the real scoop on how ICM was being run. I don't know how you managed to convince him, but it worked. I'm now managing the magazine and things are quickly turning around. Thank you.

I do need to discuss one thing further with you. In your last letter, you said something

*about loving me. You actually wrote the word
love. That's a serious statement that we should
discuss in depth.*

TURN AROUND MORON.

"What?" he muttered. "Turn around?"

"Yes. Turn around," Lindsey said from the doorway
of the back deck.

Jayson turned, and when he saw her, he nearly fell
over. He had to lean against the sofa for a little extra support. She was standing there completely naked.

"You're naked," he stated, unable to believe his own
eyes.

"I am. You're pretty observant." Sarcasm dripped
from her words as she grinned at him.

"Why are you naked?" he asked. "Not that I'm com-
plaining."

"Because it's Wednesday. I warned you about
Wednesdays."

He chuckled and shook his head. "Yes, you did."

He moved toward her and she put up a hand. "Wait,
we need to talk about this love business."

He put his hands on his hips to keep from grabbing
her. "Really? Right now?"

"Sure right now. Why not?"

He sighed. "Because you're naked and within touching distance. I'm not sure my brain will function correctly again for several hours."

She closed the gap between them and wrapped her

186

arms around his neck. "Then I'll do the talking." She brushed a light kiss on his lips and pulled back to look at him. "I think I love you too."

He smiled brightly. "Really?"

"Yes, that's why I burned the letters you wrote me. I don't want to take a chance on anyone ever finding them." She hugged him, then slapped his butt. "I want to be the only one that knows all your secrets."

He brushed the hair back from her face so he could look into her eyes. "Thank you."

She shook her head. "No, thank you for trusting me." Then she pulled away and grabbed his hand, leading to the room that was once her bedroom. She glanced back at him and said, "You know what? I'm really looking forward to Thursdays."

He threw back his head and laughed, then scooped her into his arms and said, "Me too, sweetheart. Me too."

Epilogue

LINDSEY SAT ON her sofa and rubbed her large round belly. She adored being pregnant, and Jayson was the most excited dad-to-be she'd ever seen. He pampered her, painted the nursery, and bought more toys than any child could ever possibly play with. She secretly wondered how many of those were really for the baby, and how many were for him. But he was happy, and that was all she cared about.

She looked around their newly-purchased home and silently gave thanks for all she had. A wonderful husband, an amazing job, and a baby on the way. They had recently celebrated yet another best seller for Jackson King, as well as a contract for two more. She couldn't imagine life being any more perfect.

The doorbell rang, and she pushed herself up off the sofa and waddled to the door. When she opened the door, she found Whitney and Caleb waiting outside.

"Oh! You're here! Please, hurry and get in here before you freeze your butts off!" She ushered in her friends and shut the door.

Whitney brushed a little snow from her lapel and then helped Caleb shrug out of his coat. "I can't believe how much it's snowed in the last week!"

"I know," said Lindsey. "I'll admit, it has me a little worried about going in to labor during a blizzard." She reached down and scratched her stomach.

"Did I hear the door?" Jayson asked as he exited his home office.

"Uncle Jayson!" Caleb ran to Jayson and jumped in his arms.

"Hey, big man!" Jayson smiled. "I'm glad to see you both!" He whispered loudly, "Auntie Lindsey needs girl time so she doesn't end up killing Uncle Jayson."

Whitney laughed. "It sounds like I got here just in time then!"

Caleb rolled his eyes. "You guys are so weird. But you're fun too, so it's okay."

The adults all smiled at each other.

Caleb squirmed, so Jayson put him down. Then the boy yelled, "Guess what! Guess What!"

Lindsey ruffled his hair. "Slow your roll, boy! You're gonna bust a button! What are you so excited about?"

Caleb looked at Whitney. "Can I tell them, Mom?"

She nodded. "Yes, you may."

He puffed up his chest proudly. "I'm gonna be a big brother!"

Lindsey screamed in excitement, and Jayson covered his ears. "Good lord, that has to be the most ear-splitting thing I've ever heard."

She pointed a finger at him. "You don't want to walk that path, mister. Hush it!"

He tried not to smile. "I'll consider it."

"Oh! Before I forget." Whitney pulled an envelope out of her purse. "This was sticking out of your mailbox at the end of the drive."

Jayson accepted the envelope and then his smile died. He looked at Lindsey and swallowed. "It's from Mark's dad."

She placed a hand on his arm and squeezed. "Maybe it's good news?"

Whitney realized it was something important and they needed some time alone. "Caleb, what do you say we go upstairs and see the baby's room? We can steal ideas from Lindsey about how to do our nursery at home."

Caleb bounced up and down again. "Yes!"

"We'll be upstairs." Whitney patted Lindsey and Jayson on the back as she followed Caleb down the hall to the stairway.

Jayson moved to the sofa and opened the letter. Lindsey sat next to him as they both read the words.

Jayson,

I know I never contact you, but I thought it was time. Something has happened that you should know about. I understand you lost contact with Dylan and Greg after the accident. Honestly, I did too. I didn't want to see any of you boys ever again. But Dylan's mom called me last week and begged me to come to the hospital. Dylan was dying of some disease I can't begin to pronounce and he was demanding I visit him. To appease his distraught mother, I went grudgingly.

Dylan told me that he was the one driving the car the night of the accident. He said he panicked when he realized what had happened. Mark was too injured to move him and Greg was pinned in place. You were the only one he could drag forward enough to get in the driver's seat. You were groggy and out of it, so you didn't protest when he moved you. Then he told the police that he'd crawled out of the back window and that's why he was on the ground when they arrived.

I owe you an apology son. So does Dylan, but he's no longer with us to do so. I believe he was indeed sorry though. He felt so guilty he had to be sure I knew the truth before he died. And now I'm passing that on to you. I hope it brings you some peace and eases at least some of your guilt. I will never get Mark back, but I know he wouldn't have wanted us all to end up angry and bitter.

I also know he would have greatly appreciated the way you take care of his old man. I've called one of those numbers you gave me. I start therapy tomorrow. Thank you.

Sincerely,
Pete Taggert

"Jayson," Lindsey whispered, "it wasn't you."

He looked at her as tears were running down his face. "It wasn't me."

She pulled him close. She could feel the relief radiate though his body as she held him. He'd been holding on to that guilt for so long, and he could finally let it go.

Before Whitney walked through that door, Lindsey had believed her life couldn't get any better, but she was wrong. That letter was a gift they could have never expected. But the last year or so had taught her that letters often held many surprises. She especially looked forward to letters from Jayson.

Acknowledgments

I can't believe this is my fifth book! It's hard to believe I've made it this far, but the truth is I'm only here thanks to God and the support of my loved ones and readers.

My family puts up with quite a lot so I can pursue this dream of mine. They are my world and I love them with all of my heart. I don't know where I'd be without you!

I appreciate my beta readers and the valuable feedback they provide to assure my books are the best they can be. You ladies are the best!

A thank you to White Rabbit Book Designs for the cover. It's so perfect for this story!

I adore Stacey's skills for making my book interiors look so amazing! Your talents have saved my sanity!

My eternal admiration goes out to my editor, Wendi, for her hard work and helping me stay on schedule despite the craziness in my life in recent months.

A special hug and thanks to my friend Gladys. Thanks for hanging with me when I was at the end of my rope.

As always, I owe a huge thanks to you, the reader. Without you I'd have no reason to keep at this. Thanks to you I have pages and pages of story ideas for future books that will keep me busy for many years to come.

About the Author

Amy Hale is an author, mother, and wife living in Illinois. She's always plotting new projects and writing down crazy ideas. She's a hopeless romantic and adores all the various ways a love story can be told. Amy also loves mystery, humor, suspense, and other action filled stories, so her goal is to blend the action with romance and keep you on your toes.

Her husband and kids are the center of her universe, although her cat believes otherwise. She also loves reading, music, and photography. When she's not writing or reading, Amy can be found watching MST3K movies with her kids, or enjoying the scenery fly by from the back of her husband's motorcycle.

BE SURE TO SIGN UP FOR AMY'S NEWSLETTER ON HER WEBSITE, SO YOU DON'T MISS THE LATEST UPDATES AND ANNOUNCEMENTS.

YOU CAN FIND AMY IN THE FOLLOWING PLACES:

WEBSITE: WWW.AUTHORAMYHALE.COM

FACEBOOK: WWW.FACEBOOK.COM/ AUTHORAMYHALE

TWITTER: @AUTHORAMYHALE

INSTAGRAM: WWW.INSTAGRAM.COM/ AUTHORAMYHALE

Other Books by
amy hale

Ulterior Motives

Catching Whitney

The Shadows Trilogy
Shadows of Jane, Book One
Shadows of Deception, Book Two

Coming Soon

Shadows of Deliverance, The Shadows Trilogy, Book Three

34829708R00114

Made in the USA
Middletown, DE
06 September 2016